SEASONS
of
Change

SEASONS of Change

DEBORAH BORMAN • GINNY GRAHAM
BARB HOWE • KAREN INGLE • LIZ KIMMEL
MARIANNE MCDONOUGH • JANET OLIVER
DONALD ROOME • J.B. SISAM • BARB WINFIELD

MINNEAPOLIS, MINNESOTA

INTRODUCTION

The Minnesota Christian Writers Guild is a not-for-profit organization that began nearly 70 years ago and is dedicated to helping writers in all stages of their careers take their craft to the next level.

This book, *Seasons of Change*, is dedicated to all writers who desire to share the good news of Jesus Christ through their written words.

Each story is based in the beautiful state of Minnesota and reflects upon some aspect of seasons – whether it relates to life, sports, or the calendar. Life without change would not be life. It normal, continual, and expected. Our hope throughout remains in Jesus, who will be with us through our trials and joys in every season.

We pray you come to treasure each story in this powerful anthology.

For more information about our organization, visit
MNCHRISTIANWRITERS.COM

Contents

SEASONS *of* Change

WATERCOLOR SKY

by Deborah Borman

Deborah Borman lives in Minnesota with her husband and achieved empty-nester status as of 2021. Graduating from Gustavus Adolphus with degrees in Psychology/Criminal Justice, Deborah worked in social work before staying at home to homeschool their three children and care for her husband after his stroke in 2009.

Deborah has written devotionals for *With God I Will Not Fear,* to be published early 2023 by Chosen Books, as well as a 21-day devotional for staff serving at *Joni and Friends Ministry Family Retreats.* She also enjoys writing middle grade and young adult fiction with themes of redemption and hopes to help young people experience the joy of reading.

Recent highlights in Deborah's life have been trips to London with her two daughters and Washington D.C. with her son. She also loves meeting with other women, guitar music, and an occasional rousing game of table tennis.

Please contact her at deb@jbsc.com.

ONE

"Keep your eye out for deer!"

Excitement tingled through Sami's tired but gloriously-tense body as her dad spoke the familiar words and switched on the Chrysler's high beams. The July sun had already set, and the tall, dark-shadowed pines lining the narrow highway signaled the final twenty miles to her grandparents' home north of Bemidji. Inspired by her dad's words and thinking he hoped to see deer as much as she did, the eager ten-year-old took her position as "sentinel-on-the-backseat-hump." She stared intently into the spray of light illuminating the gravel and grassy ditches ahead.

Twenty miles later and no deer sightings to show for it, the car tires slowly crunched the last loose rocks as Sami's dad turned off the unpaved road and onto the smooth cement driveway of Grandpa Leo's garage. From a side door stepped a trim, salt-and-pepper-haired man wearing a blue mechanic's suit, wiping engine grease from his hands with an oil-stained towel.

"Well, there ye be," her grandpa greeted them amiably as the four travelers unfurled their stiff bodies from the car like butterflies from a cocoon.

"Grandpa, we didn't see any deer!" Sami complained, first to escape the packed backseat and run to meet him.

"Doesn't surprise me," Grandpa Leo replied, tossing aside the rag and giving her a hug. "There's been a fire on the reservation, and they're running a little skittish. You might not see any while you're here." Grandpa Leo always spoke very calmly. Known to be somewhat of an "animal-whisperer," he enjoyed carrying on conversations with the birds, raccoon, fox, and deer that shared his 40-acre property in the Minnesota Northwoods. Even the squirrels and chipmunks received his kind attention, and Sami would often hear him say in his soft, low voice, "Well, hello there, little one. How are you today?" He'd continue on with some small talk about the weather and whatever else he thought relevant in the little critter's life.

Hearing Grandpa Leo's news about the deer, Sami's small shoulders drooped. She remembered her embarrassment during their visit last summer when she had come around the back corner of the house to find a beautiful white-tailed doe standing 20 yards away, munching on some mowed grass. In her excitement, she had yelled to her grandpa to come see it. By the time he had reached the door of the garage, the frightened creature had bounded away.

"You need to stay very quiet and calm, or you will scare them off," Grandpa Leo had told her gently, which of course she knew and felt both embarrassed and sad but mostly embarrassed. The excitement of seeing a deer so close had gotten the best of her. For the rest of their week up north that summer, Sami kept a lookout on the edges of the woods and the nearby fields of alfalfa and wildflowers. Much to her disappointment, however, she didn't see another deer their entire visit. Regret tucked itself like a sharp cocklebur deep in her sensitive heart.

But this was a new summer, and Sami's hopes of seeing a deer this year were as high as the bright new moon. As her mom and dad unpacked the car, Sami and her younger brother Jesse helped carry their things to the double-wide trailer their grandparents called home. With arms and heart full, Sami walked slowly down the cement sidewalk, pausing at the spot she had seen the doe the previous summer. With a whisper, she prayed to Jesus for another chance to see the gentle animals she loved so much. She hoped to redeem last summer's mistake and show her grandpa that she could stay calm like him and show the animals she was their friend.

Two

Every morning that week, Sami woke up early, trying to catch a glimpse of deer in her grandparents' large front yard and dense woods across the dirt road. From an east window, she checked the salt licks tucked in the woods near the house; then, running the length of the mobile home, she searched the far west meadow from Grandma's small kitchen window.

Once done with breakfast, other activities occupied her mind. Fishing was one of her favorites. When it was time to go, Sami and her brother would both don their somewhat-too-tight, faded orange life vests—being careful not to pinch any skin as they clicked the buckles—and race down the long steep hill to the dock. With their dad at the motor and their mom holding the boat, Sami and Jesse would gingerly climb to their assigned seat, being careful not to rock the boat too much. The four of them spent hours fishing for sunnies on the remote lake, watching the fireflies land on their poles, putting worms on the hook, and chewing long pieces of red licorice until the next sudden dip of the bobber. Sami loved the quiet lake with just her family and no other boats around.

Back on land, there were turtle eggs to watch hatch and animal tracks to find and follow. A porcupine slept high in a nearby birch tree. How far can they throw their quills? She wondered. She gave the tree a wide berth to be safe. Sami also enjoyed the bumpy jeep rides into the backwoods to see her dad and Grandpa's deer stands, following old tire ruts with grass as high as the Jeep's hood. She and Jesse liked to pull the thick blades and make funny sounds blowing it between their thumbs as the Jeep slowly drove by. When she wasn't watching for deer, Sami kept her eye out for the small, spider-like wood ticks that liked to jump from the grass and hide in her clothes. One summer, she woke up in the morning with a brown tick stuck to her eyelid. Sami's mom lit a match, blew it out, then touched the hot match tip to the tick's hard, flat body. This had the desired effect of making the tick back its head out of Sami's skin, only to meet its own well-justified end. Sami was pretty sure wood ticks were not in God's original plan when He called everything He had made "good."

Down the road from her grandparents' place stood the property's abandoned, one-story farmhouse. Grandpa Leo used the wood building next to it as a repair shop. People from miles around would bring their broken engines—boat motors, snow-mobiles, power tools, tractors—and Sami's grandpa would fix them for free. At least he offered to fix them for free. It wasn't uncommon for him to tote home various "donations" from his satisfied customers—a hunk of venison, a beautiful ring-necked pheasant, bags of tomatoes and ears of corn, or even beer. He'd lay the items on the kitchen table and say with a grin, "I brought us home some supper, Ma." Sami and her brother enjoyed walking down the gravel road to see Grandpa working in his shop. That is until the inevitable lone black horsefly began droning around their heads, sending both Sami and her brother sprinting down the dusty road, arms flailing wildly. Horseflies were another questionable invention, in Sami's humble opinion.

On rainy days, the family spent their time playing checkers or Yahtzee, eating Grandma's cinnamon sugar donuts, and listening to stories about the "olden days" or the latest neighborhood news. Apparently, the Nurdstrands weren't talking to the Nordstroms because the Nordstroms' cow had ambled into the Nurdstrands' garden or something like that. Sami couldn't keep everything straight. Her grandma and grandpa were also members of *The Elks Lodge,* a local club that organized various social and charitable events in the surrounding counties. The men were called *elks,* and each woman member a *doe.* For some reason, it reminded Sami of Fred and Wilma in the *Flintstones* cartoon, but she kept that thought to herself. Eventually, she would quietly excuse herself and go read from Grandma's set of *Reader's Digest* or play songs like "Que Sera Sera," and "Raindrops Keep Falling On My Head" on Grandma's small electric organ. To Sami, vacation up north was a carefree, happy time.

When the glorious week came to an end, however, Sami still had not sighted a single deer. As they loaded suitcases into the car and said their goodbyes, Grandpa Leo put his arm around her. He didn't say anything, but she knew he understood. She glanced up gratefully before climbing into the car, waving back at him as they drove off.

THREE

The beautiful Minnesota fall came quickly—and with it schoolwork, piano lessons, leaf piles, and slumber parties with friends. Sami forgot about the deer. Then, one November morning at breakfast, her dad reminded her he was heading up to Grandma and Grandpa's land to go deer hunting.

"I'll be back on Friday, Sam," he told her as he put the final items into his duffel bag, packing a sandwich and apple for lunch on the way up. "You and Jesse have a good week with your mom. Don't forget to help with the dishes."

"Yes, Dad." Sami gave her brother a big-sister-look that said, "This means you too, bub." She drank the last of her milk. "Say hi for me," she sang to her dad, giving him a quick kiss goodbye. Then, grabbing her books and Hardy Boys lunch box, she ran out the front door to catch the waiting school bus.

The school week passed slowly. Sami missed her dad when he was gone. Finally, still clearing the last of Friday's supper dishes, Sami heard the familiar squeak of the Chrysler's brakes as the car slowed and pulled into the driveway.

"Dad's home!" she yelled to her mom and brother, the last of the dirty plates rattling as she quickly set them in the sink. Too excited to wait for a response, Sami ran out the front screen door, bounding down the front steps and towards the driveway.

Suddenly she stopped. There, on the top of the car, lay the lifeless body of a large white-tailed buck. Its gray coat lay flat and dull in the evening dusk. Two smooth antlers sprouted like tree branches from the top of its large, still head, and its long legs hung limply over the back windshield. But most troubling to Sami were its eyes—large glassy pools set in a vacant stare. They shone oddly as they reflected the artificial indoor light. They weren't looking at her. They weren't looking at anything. Sami's mouth opened, and let out a choked cry before she could stop it. She stood perfectly still in a mix of anguish and fascination at the disturbing vision.

Sami's dad had come around the front of the car, ready to be met with the usual hug from his happy daughter. Seeing her standing there motionless, he walked quickly to her, still in his camouflage jacket and pants, and put his arms around her.

"Sam, I know this is hard," he said gently. "It is always hard to see death, even the death of an animal who will provide food for us."

Trembling in the cold fall air, Sami didn't know what to say. Warm tears began to roll slowly down her cheeks. She remembered how badly she had wanted to see a deer this past summer. But not like this.

"I'm sorry you had to see the deer this way," her dad quietly continued, intuitively knowing her thoughts. He took her hand and led her to the front steps, where they sat down together. "I'm taking it tomorrow to the person who will process the meat for us, but they were already closed for today. I can tell you that it did not suffer. But your tears are good and right tears because death means saying goodbye to something beautiful and good. We just have to remember that God promises a day when death will be no more and our tears will be only happy tears."

Sami wasn't so sure she understood it all, but she wanted to and slowly nodded her head. Then, taking one last look at the body, she wiped her tears with her sleeve, and together she and her dad went into the house.

FOUR

In the weeks ahead, as snow began to fall and the Christmas season came and went, Sami thought about her dad's words, and the ache in her heart for the beautiful buck gradually lessened. Grandma Marie and Grandpa Leo drove the long journey to the cities for the New Year's holiday, which meant a rare gathering with cousins and a huge bucket of Kentucky Fried Chicken, Grandpa Leo's treat. Enjoying her drumstick, Sami wondered why all food didn't taste this "finger lickin' good."

Through the rest of the winter, Sami and her grandma kept in touch through short letters. For her grandpa's birthday in March, Sami recorded a couple of classical songs she could play on the piano and sent the tape to him. In her next letter, Grandma Marie told her how much Grandpa Leo enjoyed it.

"Your grandpa hasn't been feeling well," Grandma wrote in her perfect handwriting on the pink stationery. "But he listened to the beautiful music you played with happy tears running down his face. Thank you so much, honey, for brightening his day and mine."

When Sami's dad heard this, he told her that Grandpa Leo had been a very good violinist as a young man. But at the age of 24, he had gone to war and fought in the battle of Okinawa, one of the fiercest battles of World War II. Sami's dad had only heard him play the violin once. If anyone ever asked Grandpa Leo about his music or the war, he would just say, "I've put many things behind me," and talk about something else. Still, Sami was glad the piano music had made her grandpa happy.

The winter months passed, bringing the warm winds of April and sweet fragrances of spring. Sami loved that the days were getting longer. Finally, there was more time to play outside, and the end of school was finally in sight.

One early April evening, as the four of them were finishing a meal of Shake-N-Bake pork chops, au gratin potatoes, and canned green beans, the phone rang. Sami's dad got up from his chair and crossed the kitchen to answer it.

"Oh hey, Mom," he said, wiping the corner of his mouth with his napkin. His voice changed. "Mom? What is it?"

Everyone stopped mid-chew, hearing his alarm. But Sami's dad had quickly walked into the next room, pulling the long, coiled telephone cord around the door with him. Minutes later, he walked back into the kitchen, hung up the phone slowly, and came to the table where they all sat very still, filled with dread.

"It's Grandpa Leo," he said. His voice broke as he told them the difficult news.

Grandpa Leo had been taken by ambulance to the Beltrami

County hospital in Bemidji with severe chest pains. A neighbor had driven Grandma along the winding country roads to the hospital. The paramedics tried to help Grandpa during the twenty-minute ride. By the time they arrived at the emergency room, he had passed away.

Their dad knelt between Sami and Jesse's chairs. Putting his arms around them, he held his children close as together they wept.

The next few weeks were a blur. Sami's dad took the day off work and brought Grandma to the cities to stay with them. Arrangements were made for Grandpa's body. There would be no funeral, but Grandpa's ashes would be spread on their property up north. Flower arrangements and sympathy cards poured in from the countless people who had been touched by Grandpa Leo's generosity and kindness. The flowers were shared, and the cards read with both smiles and tears, each one receiving a personal response in Grandma's beautiful handwriting.

When the first week of May came, Grandma Marie quietly announced that she was ready to return to her home. Sami's dad drove his mom on the long trip, staying with her for a few days. The plan was made for the whole family to return at the usual time in July. Then they would spread Grandpa's ashes.

Sami's fifth-grade year ended, and before she knew it, it was time for their trip up north. Normally she couldn't wait to be at her grandparents' place. But now, instead of anticipation, all she felt was dread.

"I know it will be hard at first." Her father comforted her

the morning of their trip. "But Jesus will be with us, and His Word promises that He is near the brokenhearted. I am praying that He gives you a special comfort when we are up there." Sami nodded, but she wasn't sure how even God could ease the sadness she felt, weighing on her chest like a two-ton stone. The fresh grief seemed to press the old thorn of regret even deeper inside her. Now she would never have the joy of seeing a deer with her grandpa. The thought was almost more than she could bear.

The five-and-a-half-hour ride to Grandma's was quiet, despite their mom's attempts to distract them with an unusual amount of their favorite snacks and a few half-hearted attempts of "If I Had A Hammer" and "Take Me Out to the Ball Game," neither of which got much response. Even her brother Jesse sat quietly in the back seat with a baseball hat pulled low over his eyes, staring out the window.

Because it was still daytime, Sami's dad did not say his customary, "Keep your eye out for deer." Instead, as the car pulled onto the concrete driveway, tears came to Sami's eyes as the familiar figure of her grandpa did not step out from the garage to welcome them. Instead, Grandma Marie walked to them along the sidewalk from the house, smiling through her tears, arms open to give each of them a big hug.

"Come inside," she encouraged them, her arm around Jesse. "Just leave your things for now." Entering the house solemn and empty-handed, the family was met with the delicious smell of Grandma's chicken and dumplings. And although Sami felt slightly guilty for being hungry, she ate all that was on her plate and even a little extra. Once dessert was finished, she finally let herself look around the place more closely. Seeing a picture of Grandpa Leo on the living room wall made the thorn in her heart throb sharply once again.

"Tomorrow, we will all get up at sunrise and spread Grandpa's ashes in the west meadow," Sami's father told them before they had left the table. He had brought in their bags during dessert. "Let's all get to bed so we can get up and be ready."

Sami headed to the bedroom and put her pajamas on slowly. She got under the covers and stared at the white paneled ceiling. Oh, how she dreaded the thought of saying goodbye to her grandpa. She was still wondering how she would make it through the next day when she drifted off to sleep.

FIVE

Sami opened her eyes. The house was quiet and still. She stood on the bed, pushing Grandma's white lace curtains aside, and peeked out the high bedroom window. The sky above the tall pines looked like a beautiful watercolor painting, with rosy pink swirls blending into layers of soft pastels of violet, purple, and blue. A light gray mist hung low over the grass surrounding the house.

Dressing quickly, Sami found her tennis shoes by the back door and quietly made her way down the patio steps and towards the meadow. As she walked around the corner of the house, she stopped. In front of her, standing in the morning mist, stood a lovely white-tailed doe and two spotted fawns. Catching Sami's scent, the doe lifted her graceful head, tail and ears pointed high, body tense. Sami held her body as still as possible, remembering her grandpa's words. She waited for what seemed an eternity. Then, keeping her voice low and friendly, she looked down at the grass in front of her and gently spoke.

"Well, hello, little mama," she said calmly, her heart pounding so hard she thought for sure the doe would hear it and run off. "What a beautiful family you have. Are you enjoying your breakfast?" Sami slowly lifted her gaze again, being careful not to move.

The doe stared at Sami with eyes of dark amber glass. The two fawns, sensing their mother's alarm, had stopped eating and now also stared at her, all three animals as still as statues. Not a muscle twitched. Sami held her breath and tried her best to match their stillness.

Suddenly, to Sami's great relief and joy, the doe bent her slender neck and resumed eating the thick grass. The two fawns followed in unison. Sami let out her breath slowly, and for the next five minutes, watched as the three deer peacefully grazed in the front yard, stepping slowly through the morning dew. Their coats were the color of warm caramel, the fawns a soft tan with cream-colored spots, and the doe's a pretty auburn brown. Then, as the rising sun's rays touched the nearby pine tops, birds awakened and began filling the still morning air with tweets and whistles and an epiphany of a new song. The beauty of the scene all around her deeply comforted Sami's soul. All she could do was watch in wonder and try to soak in the peace of it all.

Gradually, the doe made her way across the front yard, grazing as she went, the two fawns close behind her. Reaching the edge of the woods, she stopped and raised her head. Then, like three morning apparitions stepping silently into another world, the silent family blended into the tall forest and was gone.

Sami stood for a few moments, keeping her eyes fixed on the tall grass where the deer had disappeared. Oblivious to her presence, the forest birds twittered, warbled, and tweeted in unaffected conversation. To the east, the sun's orange orb had now risen fully above the horizon, and the feathery grasses of the west meadow glowed in the morning light.

Like one awakening from a dream, Sami slowly began to hear the sounds of muffled conversation and clanging kitchen dishes from inside the house. She sighed and turned to walk slowly to the back of the house and up the patio steps. How she wished she could tell her Grandpa what she had just seen and how she had stayed calm as he had told her. She missed him so much.

At that same moment, as she stood reaching for the screen door, she heard the tender voice of her Grandpa Leo—whether in her mind or in her heart or in the morning wind, she did now know. Soft and low, full of love came the familiar words, "Well, there ye be...." A deep current of peace washed over Sami, and she felt the sharp thorn of regret and grief dislodge and float away.

"Thank you, Grandpa," she whispered. "And thank you, Jesus." Then, looking over her shoulder at the west meadow, Sami smiled and walked into the house.

A Dog Named Money

by Ginny Graham

Ginny Graham's writing touches on the complications faced by widows. And, in the case of this short story, widowers. Spouses are an interdependent team who each find meaning and function in the other. Her writing seeks to touch on the complexities faced by those experiencing the loss of a spouse.

With a degree in business administration, Ginny has a background in sales and marketing and experience as a small-business owner. She now writes full-time.

When Ginny is not writing, she serves as a Sunday School teacher, a choir member, and in women's ministries at her church. Her hobbies include writing, reading, hiking, sewing, gardening, and horseback riding. At the top of her list, she enjoys the treasure of spending time with her family. She is a widowed mother of two sons. God has blessed her with two daughters-in-law and eight grandchildren. She lives in Pine Island, Minnesota.

ONE

For the love of money is a root of all kinds of evil. Some people, eager for money, have wandered from the faith and pierced themselves with many griefs.

— *I TIMOTHY 6:10 (NIV)*

Ward Bluffington didn't know where the dog came from or why he answered to the name of Money. He just showed up during a blustery November day—the kind that reminds you of fall chores you should finish before the snow flies. And chores you'd rather ignore, like getting rid of a dead tree. Daniel Swanson, that upstart of a next-door neighbor's child, reminded him he had agreed to pay half to remove a tree that fell into Ward's yard.

Ward glared at his pint-sized nine-year-old neighbor. "What do you think I am? Made of MONEY?"

A dog came out of nowhere, nudged Ward's leg, and wagged his tail to beat the band.

"Is that your dog?" Ward scowled at Daniel.

"No, never seen him before," Daniel said. "But I think his name is Money."

The dog wheeled and tried to lick the boy's face.

"Money? No dog's named Money."

The dog barked and pressed its shoulder against Ward's leg in response.

"Someone should call animal protection and get rid of him." Ward shoved his knee into the dog to push it aside. "Now, why does your dad want so much to get rid of that dead tree?"

"The tree service wanted five hundred dollars, but dad found a friend who charged a hundred and fifty. Your half is seventy-five. You told him to get rid of it, and you would pay half. Remember?"

"I'm retired, but I still have a mind." Ward scratched his head of gray, thinning hair. "Wait here."

The storm door creaked in protest when Ward yanked it open. Huffing, he jiggled the knob of the old inner door and pushed through it. After five minutes, he returned and handed Daniel the cash.

"Thanks, Mr. Bluff."

"That's Bluffington."

"Oh, sorry, Mr. Bluffington." Daniel flew down the steps and slapped his leg. "Money, wanna come home with me?"

The blur of a boy and a dog raced across the yard. Still standing on his front porch, Ward shook his head as he heard Daniel fling open his front door and call the dog. "Come on, Money, it's okay. Come inside."

With a mad dash, Money cleared the Swansons' threshold.

"Mom! Can we keep him? Look at the dog I found."

Daniel's voice echoed down the street.

"Would someone please close the door?" A baby's startled cry punctuated Daniel's mother's pleading to keep the cold outdoors.

Ward plodded toward his computer in his former dining room. A computer desk replaced the old dining room table, the only change to the home's interior since his wife had died.

Daniel's words seared through him. "Mr. Bluff. Humph. Wonder if that's what people always called me behind my back." He spoke aloud. He did that frequently. "Maybe that's why I barely survived selling used cars. Never made it big."

But he'd made it big now—a day trader. Retirement felt good. In his younger days, he'd loved cars, fixing and fine-tuning them, but eventually, it became a life of plodding through a job that held little interest for him. Then, five years ago, a friend introduced him to the world of trading. A few mistakes. A few wins. Then he leveled off and watched, amazed as his retirement account grew. His portfolio hit his goal of a million last year—time for a new goal. With a smirk, he headed for his computer. He couldn't wait to see where the markets had landed after closing, and he had just wasted fifteen minutes. He opened his laptop. His heart raced up and down along with the multi-colored indicators of exponential moving averages.

Following a possible turn in the market, he recognized an opportunity for a short-scalp trade. His diligence paid off. A few minutes later, he leaned back and closed his eyes. A dog barked. Children's cries sifted through the walls of his poorly insulated home. With the racket in the yard next door, who could concentrate?

Ward peeked through his dining room drapes. That dratted dog was still there, jumping around Daniel as he raked leaves into a pile. His little sister, Zoey, added scant leaves into his stack with her broken rake. Money ran through leaves and demolished their pile. Zoey stopped raking, threw leaves in the air, and shrieked when Money jumped high to catch them.

Two

The next day, Saturday, Ward took a break from his laptop to prepare for the fast-approaching winter. Filling the snowblower with gas and locating the shovels took the wind out of him. Maybe he should rethink what the doctors said about a pacemaker. They compared his body to a car with the parts wearing out. The mere thought made his blood boil. As if he were an Indy 500 race car. And he certainly didn't want to pay for race-car-quality upkeep on his heart.

Working in front of his shed, he brushed leaves from a bench and collapsed. Winter. On its way, and nothing could stop it. The winter of his life. Nothing could stop that, either. The children's laughter next door rose to squeal pitch. Fool kids, rolling in the leaves with that dog again. Great. They spotted him.

Bundled in her jacket with the hood tied securely under her chin, Zoey trundled across the backyard to the bench where Ward rested.

"Hi, Mr. Bluff." Zoey hopped up on the other end of the bench.

Ward wasn't about to correct Zoey. After all, he had had a little girl once. Boys reminded him of himself when he was young, selfish little brutes. Ah, but little girls. They could wiggle right into your heart.

"I think Money's ours. Nobody claimed him yet."

"I don't doubt that."

At the mention of his name, Money perked up his ears. He stood next to Daniel, who stuffed leaves into a garbage bag.

"Money's so cute."

Money bounded across the yard. He stopped beside Zoey for a caress, then stuck his nose against Ward's knee. A quick shuffle of Ward's leg and Money retreated.

Ward heard Zoey sniffle. "I don't know what we're going to do." She weaved her fingers into the thick honey-colored hair around Money's neck. "Mom has to go to work Monday, and Paisley's going to daycare. With Daniel and me in school, there won't be anyone to take care of Money during the day."

"What? Why would your mom take the baby to daycare? She always gets home before your dad leaves for work."

"Dad's working all day now at the restaurant. Anyway, he's going to close it down at the end of the month. He said after the shutdown, he's in over his head."

That blasted pandemic had wrecked everything. Ward made a habit of ignoring his neighbors. What they did was their own business. He told himself he didn't care what became of them, but inside he fumed over the news.

Zoey swung her legs back and forth as Money settled on the ground between her and Ward.

"I know." Zoey's face lit up. "Money could stay at your house during the day."

"No. Don't go pulling me into your problems."

"Oh please, Mr. Bluff. Pleeeze."

"No." Ward rose stiffly.

Late Monday morning, the sound of barking crescendoed next door. Ward squinted through his kitchen window. The neighbors' solution to dog sitting seemed to be putting Money on a chain during the day. Tangled in his chain, Money howled.

"Fool dog." Ward pulled on his jacket, adjusted his cap with pull-down ear muffs, and slipped into his boots.

"Easy now, Money. I'll get you loose."

Money turned his big liquid eyes on Ward and whined.

When Ward unwrapped the chain, he noticed a cut on Money's side.

"Well, you better come over and let me wash it." Ward walked toward his home. Money shook himself and obediently trotted behind.

Money stood like a soldier while Ward cleaned the wound, but flinched when he applied peroxide as a last step.

"Supposed to snow. You ever been through a winter in Minnesota, Money? Living outside? You don't even have a dog house yet." He gazed at the makeshift shelter beside the Swansons' back door. "Maybe you should sit tight till they come home."

Ward washed his hands and slapped together a sandwich for lunch. Money's eyes rotated as Ward shoveled the plate to the table. Ward half-expected him to lift one paw and go on point. Instead, the dog's eyes followed the sandwich from plate to mouth and back to plate. "Well, if you hadn't dumped your food when you pulled that chain, you'd have had lunch, too. You'll not get food off the table. Not good for dogs."

Money whined and slumped on the floor as if he understood.

Ward eyed the dog's long body. "You're too small to be a lab, probably a lab-hound mix." Ward brought a runner from the hall, and Money planted his body on the rug before Ward's motion stopped. "Don't get the idea that's your permanent bed."

Soon, snow dusted the yard. Then, at dusk that afternoon, Ward noticed lights flickering in the Swansons' house.

"Time to go home." He opened the door wide, and Money ran for Zoey, who stood at her back door holding the tangled chain.

A few minutes later, Ward answered a knock on his back door. Zoey tumbled inside.

She threw both arms around his legs. "Oh, Mr. Bluff."

"Hey, watch it. I'm an old man. I could lose my balance."

"Sorry. But thanks for taking care of Money. I just hated leaving him alone, but you're an answer to prayer." Zoey clasped her hands.

"Prayer? You pray about a dog?"

"Yes, I pray about everything. Don't you?"

"No." *She prayed about everything, huh? Prayer didn't save her dad's business. Didn't save Rosemary and little Carrie in that accident years ago.* "Now, don't go putting him on that chain anymore. Did you see the size of the cut on his side?"

"I know." Zoey hung her head and didn't move.

Ward shook his head. Now what? What was he supposed to do? *It's their problem.*

"I guess you can turn him loose in the morning and see if he wanders over here." Talking to a dog was better than talking to himself.

THREE

Early the next morning, Zoey brought Money to Ward's back door. Ward had trouble distinguishing her knock from the noise of the sleet pelting the roof.

"I think we're getting more dogs," she said.

"What?" Ward crowded them inside out of the wind. "Are you loco?"

"What's loco?"

"Never mind. What's this about more dogs?"

"I couldn't hear everything with the door closed. Mom and Dad went into their bedroom. Said they needed privacy. But I heard Dad say 'Money.' And then Mom said, 'We need more.'"

"Humph. You'd better get off to school so Money and I can get to work."

The laptop lit up.

"Money to be made." He turned as Money sat up. "Hey,

fella, do you want to make some money?"

Money's ears perked up.

"Yeah, I feel the same way." He deftly clicked his mouse on his Fibonacci retracement tool. "Let's see, your favorite dog food. What company makes that?"

Money cocked his head.

"Purina owned by Nestlé. Go figure. No, too stable. We need volatility. Let's find a startup. Here's a sleepy company that's likely to come awake. Best Friend Dog Food and Supplies. A dog's their best friend? Kind of sad. Unless it's true. Who's your best friend, Money?"

Money moaned as he plopped his chin over his front paws.

"I'll put one-hundred dollars into your account. You'd better make enough through trading to pay for your dog food. Dog food's not cheap, you know."

The ever-changing graphs and prices flipping in real-time mesmerized him. Definitely headed for a bull market.

Ward glanced at Money stretched out on the rug by his office chair. "How's it feel to be a trader?"

Money's tail thumped, and his eyes met Ward's.

"Wait. What's going on? Forget your hundred. With today's activity, I could make a mint."

At 3 p.m., a knock at the back door interrupted his frenzied day of trading.

"Coming!" Ward yelled and snarled at the computer. "Drat. Now the markets are closed. No time to analyze results."

He opened the door to Daniel's blanched, wild-eyed face." Mr. Bluff, could you keep Money for a while longer? We're headed to the hospital. Zoey had an accident at school."

"Zoey? What happened?"

"Yeah, slipped on the ice. Or got shoved." Daniel blinked

and swallowed hard. "Hit the back of her head."

"A concussion?"

"Dunno."

Ward stared at the frozen landscape. "Anything . . . " His voice trailed off.

"All we can do is pray, Mom says."

Pray. That word again. Didn't they know he had stopped years ago?

"I gotta go. Dad's waiting." Daniel spun away, ran across the yard, and jumped into his dad's restaurant van. Ward grabbed Money's collar as he tried to follow.

"Not yet, fella."

Ward sat down slowly at his kitchen table. He stared at the empty chair where Rosemary had always sat. Had forty years passed since then? He looked around. She had been so proud when she'd papered these kitchen walls. Pale green stripes alternated with stripes of muted roses. Pleasing but subdued, just like Rosemary. Why would he ever change anything? Her Bible still sat on the bookshelf next to the phone book. He had never had the heart to store it away. He buried his head in his folded arms. Money whimpered.

Ward must have dozed off. Pounding on the back door aroused him at five p.m. He hobbled to the back door. Money sprang for the door and jumped at Daniel.

"They're going to keep her overnight." Daniel rubbed the dog. "Hey Money, wanna come home?"

A tear traced a line down Ward's face as he shut and locked the door.

FOUR

The next morning, a sleepy Daniel knocked on the door. Dark circles under his eyes told the story. "Nothing new," he said as he dropped Money off. Daniel flipped his hood over his uncombed hair and slouched across the yard, a forlorn black-jacketed figure amid increasing snow blending with their white house. Another black and white winter day.

Ward bundled up and chipped at the ice on his back steps. Once the snow stopped, a little salt and a little sun should take care of the ice. He did the same for his front porch while Money stared through a low window and barked.

"Don't know what you're barking about," he grumbled as he entered. "I'm doing all the work." But he rubbed Money behind the ears.

He sank into the kitchen chair and waited for his heart rate to go down. Ward's gaze wandered to Rosemary's Bible. Across the table, the same empty chair seemed to stare at him. Why was Rosemary on his mind so much? He missed her now more than ever. She always had a way of sanding off his rough edges without saying a word. He could almost feel her gentle hand on his shoulder. Why did she and his little Carrie have to die in that accident?

And now, little Zoey?

"Money, the best thing we can do now is concentrate on making money."

Money stood at attention.

"Hey! I never got back to your dog food buy, did I?"

How could he be so negligent? He had meant to get in and get out, quick. But then, the hundred dollars was dog food compared to his windfall of profits yesterday. He smiled at his own wit and settled into his office chair. He then sucked in his breath. He clutched his chest in horror, then in total bafflement.

By noon, Ward was peacefully sipping coffee at the kitchen table when Daniel banged on the back door.

"Zoey's home." Daniel managed a one-sided smirk. Probably the closest thing to a smile that a nine-year-old could produce for his little sister.

"Thank God."

Daniel's eyes widened. "Yeah. Doctor says she'll be okay with rest."

Money slipped through the door and led their way home.

The phone rang. Ward stepped sprightly across the room, feeling stronger than he'd felt in years.

"Jensen?" He barked into the phone. "Got my message?"

Ward frowned.

"Don't give me that client privilege jazz. How long have

you known me? I just want the amount. Do I need to come down there?"

His hand touched Rosemary's open Bible as he hung up.

Ward parked and entered the bank. It was a long walk from the parking lot, but he wasn't about to get a handicap sticker. He paused at the entrance and wondered how much longer his ticker would hold up. Maybe he should make an appointment with the doc.

The bank building still sported its update from twenty years ago, with no facelift. That gave Ward a keen feeling of satisfaction because he'd voted down the new president's relocation plans. Everyone had agreed with Ward. Sensible thing to do, the bank saved a ton of money. He walked past the teller cages to the offices.

His banker, Jensen, stood in his office doorway and motioned to Ward. "Good to see you, Ward." He closed the door behind them. At Ward's curt nod, Jensen dispensed with further social conventions.

"A rather strange request. Sorry I can't comply."

"Look, Jensen, I'm a trustee."

"Doesn't matter—"

"Well, how about if you pull their loan up on your computer and I accidentally look over your shoulder?"

"Ward, there are laws."

"Fine." Ward pulled out a checkbook, wrote quickly, and handed a check to Jenson.

Jensen shook his head. "Ward—"

"I know. You're ready to call the psych ward. Don't bother."

An anniversary clock ticked on the credenza. Ward crossed his arms and leaned back. "Okay, I'll level with you. As embarrassing as it is to admit, I live next door to the Swansons and watch their dog during the day. Just for kicks, I made a financial investment for the dog. You know, fast in, fast out, earn enough to pay for his dog food."

"Ward," Jensen chuckled. "Only you would think of that."

"Well, instead of one hundred dollars, I accidentally keyed in one hundred thousand dollars."

Jensen let out a slow whistle. "So what happened?"

"It was two for one."

"You doubled your investment?"

"Does that check pay off their restaurant loan?"

"You know I can't tell you that." Jensen smiled.

"When you send the papers, paid in full, attach a sticky note that says, 'From Money.'"

"Huh?"

"You heard me." Ward tapped his finger to stop Jensen's scribbling. "Make that a capital M."

Better Than a Trophy Fish

by Barb Howe

BARB HOWE first ventured into the art of storytelling as a child during sleepovers with girlfriends. As an adult, she utilized these skills while working in higher education, health care, church, and freelance settings before putting her pen to several family memoirs and conducting community education classes on the art of memoir writing. When she became a grandparent, Howe considered the impact her life and writing would have on the newest member of her family. That awareness prompted her to commit to being an intentional Christian grandparent.

Currently, Howe is content editor and contributor for Christian Grandparenting Network. She has been published in Focus on the Family Clubhouse Jr. magazine, a Guideposts Book, blogs, and numerous other articles. Her first book of fiction for teens and young adults, *Stormy Encounters*, is planned to release in spring 2023.

Visit her website at barbhowe.org
or at ChristianGrandparenting.com

 facebook.com/Barb-Howe-Author

ONE

The only thing on my mind was winning a trophy. Well, that and showing Babbo I could catch one as big as he could.

Jake's my name. I have a younger sister named Jesse and parents named James (Jimmy) and Joanna (Jo) Jardinelli. They decided the "J" naming thing was a good idea for some reason. I don't entirely understand, but it makes for easy conversation starters. Well, enough of that. Fishing is the thing I want to talk about, in this case, a specific fishing event, our town's annual Firecracker Fishing Tournament. It's a summer tradition at our house.

Like always, Babbo set his sights on winning the grand prize. This year, it's a 14-foot Lund fishing boat. No, not one of those fancy ones with built-in live wells and places to stash your poles and tackle. I'm talking about a simple aluminum job with a 10hp outboard motor mounted on the back. Babbo always wanted a fishing boat, but as soon as he came close to saving enough money to buy one, something more important came up. First, there was the down payment on our house, and then there was me being born, a new car, my sister being born prematurely, braces for my crooked teeth, and, well, you get the picture.

Mamma was good at putting a kibosh on Babbo's boat fantasies with a few words, something like, "Jimmy, we're having a baby," or "Jimmy, we need a car more than we need a boat," or "Jimmy, we need a new furnace."

Last year, Babbo came in a close second to the grand prize, a mere three ounces short of the winner's haul of largemouth and smallmouth bass. He picked up some nice trophies and awards twice in other contests for bringing in the most fish, and twice for the biggest single fish. But he never won the grand prize of the largest total catch by weight, and it bugged him. He was pretty sure this would be his year. I could tell by the way he waved his hands around when he talked, which he does a lot, being he's an Italian American.

"Did you load the bait bucket into the truck?"

"Yeah, Babbo. That was the first thing on my list."

"Good. How about those new lures we picked up yesterday?"

"Yes. I checked everything off the list you gave me when I put them in the tackle box. It's all there." I popped open the tackle box to show him it was full.

Getting ready for the Firecracker was always exciting at our house, not to mention at every house in the entire town. It's a huge party where spectators sit back and watch the contestants while eating their way through a caravan of offerings from food trucks that ring the judging area. Then there are kiddie games and a rock band to keep the energy level running at full speed. But by far, the most fun is had by the fishermen, of which I'm the most determined, next to Babbo, of course.

As a 16-year-old, this is my first time competing in the adult division side by side with my father in a rental boat. Theoretically, we could both get our wishes from the same contest: him winning the grand prize and me getting at least one fish that's bigger than any in his catch. It would be pretty cool to get our picture in the local paper for that kind of outcome. So with that carrot dangling in my imagination like a prized lure, I helped Babbo get ready. We filled the tackle box ahead of time because we didn't want anything to slow us down from hitting the lake when the starting horn sounded. I fell asleep dreaming about the colossal fish I would handily yank out of the lake. Think Jonah and the whale size.

Then it happened. A huge thunderstorm jarred me out of bed at 3 a.m. I stared out of the window in disbelief while Babbo scanned the local weather reports. Instead of clearing skies, our friendly meteorologist warned that conditions would worsen. Sporting a toothy smile, he advised that we might even get a tornado out of this band of dense, fun-killing clouds. We both wondered if the tournament organizers would cancel the fishing contest. That never happened in its twenty-year history.

"We're already registered. Let's go to the lake and see what's happening," Babbo said. "We might at least get one of the goodie bags sponsors put together for participants."

Those bags were packed with new lures and artificial baits donated by local sporting goods stores. Some of my best ones came from them, and it would be super nice to have a few extras as backup. Plus, it's cool to have some freebies to give away to the rookie fishermen we meet at the pier during the summer. That said, not everyone in our house was as excited about this fishing tournament as I was.

Two

"Are you two going out in this weather?" Mamma called from the kitchen where she and Jesse cleaned up after breakfast.

Mamma was not as adventurous as Babbo and I were. Storms, especially the electrical variety, set her into a frenzy checking the emergency kit, testing the flashlights, shushing us every time a new weather alert flashed on her phone—nothing like her normal in-control self.

"Yeah, Jo. We'll probably be back in a few minutes," Babbo said. He tossed a cooler with water and snacks into the back of the pickup. "Do you two want to come along?"

"Not now," Mamma said. "We'll come over if the weather clears up. Call me when you get there."

Luckily, Mamma knew there was no way to talk Babbo out of a fishing tournament; otherwise, we might never get out of the house. But just in case Mamma changed her mind on that one, Babbo and I hopped into the pickup and took off. But, of course, we both left our phones on the kitchen counter in our hurry to leave. No matter, plenty of other fishermen had phones.

When we got to the lake, the parking lots were packed with pickups, campers, and every other kind of vehicle capable of hauling a fishing boat. We found a space some distance from the lake and worked our way to the boat rental dock where the Alumicraft we reserved was ready and waiting. Turns out, the storms veered to the north and the sky was beginning to clear.

"Let's get going, Jake. There are already a dozen boats out there," Babbo said as he scanned the lake.

"Everything's loaded," I said. "Did that while you were signing for the boat. I even borrowed someone's phone to call Mamma. They'll meet us at the awards table after the contest."

We puttered along to our secret spot next to an island where we'd been landing some big ones lately. Except, today we found out our spot was not so secret. Seven other boats lined up along the big dropoff where the best bass in the lake hung out. Babbo crunched his lips together the way he always does when he's trying to figure out a Plan B.

"Let's try the lagoon," he said. "Sometimes bass like to hide in the weeds when the weather changes like it did today."

"But Babbo, we never catch the really big ones there," I pleaded.

"Well Jake, we can ask the Lord to save the biggest ones for us."

So we did. Right there in the middle of the lake. Babbo just set his pole on the side of the boat and bowed his head.

"Dear Lord, You know how much a new boat means to me and a trophy means to Jake. So, Father, I ask that You fill our boat with fish like You filled Peter's boat when You called him to follow You."

No doubt about it, Babbo was asking for one gigantic miracle. I was curious to see how God would answer. He sometimes gives a "Yes" when we least expect it and a "No" when we try to own the outcome. Thirty minutes later, we still had nothing. I was getting impatient, but Babbo kept casting his line out toward the lily pads near the shore.

"Shouldn't we try another spot?" I asked, reluctantly whirling my line off the opposite side of the boat near a clump of cattails.

"Maybe. Let me give it one more cast," Babbo answered. As soon as his lure hit the water, the pole bent into an arc that could only mean one thing: a big one. "Grab the net!" he yelled.

THREE

I jammed my pole into its slot on the opposite side of the boat and hopped next to Babbo, net in hand. It took forever for him to reel the fish close enough to get a good look. It was a whopper, and it was a fighter. I lowered the net into the water and deftly lifted the biggest largemouth he had ever caught into the boat.

"Woo-hoo! Thank You, Lord," Babbo whooped.

The boat lurched. I whirled around to see my pole bent so far, I thought it would break. With one giant leap, I managed to grab it before it came loose and fell in the water. Whatever was on the line, it was determined to go deep. I reeled it in forcefully until I felt the fish weakening.

"Get the net. This is another big one."

"Steady, steady, careful it doesn't snap the line," Babbo said, in his calm way of talking.

The fish was near the boat. Babbo positioned the net while I cranked the reel, and the fish fought. Then, with one smooth motion, I brought it to the surface. It was a gigantic largemouth bass, a real beauty, if I do say so myself. Babbo snagged it with the net and swung it into the boat.

"Whoa. This one is even bigger than mine," he said. "It's gotta be a six pounder."

We measured it, then stashed it in my five-gallon aerated bucket next to an identical one with Babbo's catch. We pulled in fish nonstop for the next two hours; some were larger than our first two. Our buckets were getting crowded and the contest time was nearing the end. It was time to get back to the dock where contest judges were calculating everyone's catch before a horn blast announced the contest's conclusion.

Babbo cranked the motor. It sputtered and stopped. He cranked it again with the same result. Before giving it a third try, Babbo bowed his head in what I recognized as his silent prayer mode. The next attempt got the motor humming. I pulled the anchor and we raced the Alumicraft across the lake to the judges' stand. A dozen or so fishermen were lined up ahead of us, waiting for their tallies. Their hauls were huge. Our catch was weighed, counted, and tallied at 2:57 p.m. A loud horn signaled the end of the contest at exactly three p.m.

"Babbo, Jake," came Jesse's voice from the crowd. She sprinted toward us.

"How many did you catch?" Mamma followed at a fast trot.

"We did good, Jo," Babbo said. "But I don't know if we did good enough to win a prize."

Five judges assembled around a table in front of spectators. I never could understand why time always seems to stand still when you're waiting for something to happen. Finally, after what felt like an eternity, a young guy from the judges' team lifted a bullhorn to his mouth.

"It's time to announce the winners of the 2021 Firecracker Fishing Contest on Lake Ann Marie, Minnesota," he boomed.

There was a prize for the angler who participated the most consecutive years. That went to a 96-year-old man who grew up fishing on Lake Ann Marie. Another award went to the biggest family group in the contest. That went to the four generations and 52 members of the Olson clan. Then things got really serious.

Next up came the winners of the largest number of fish caught, the largest single fish caught, and the grand prize for the largest haul of fish by weight. The crowd was silent. Eight guys, including Babbo and me, held our collective breaths waiting to hear which of us had won.

The winner of the largest number of fish went to a twenty-something veteran, recently discharged from active duty. He sprinted to the judge's table wearing a shirt emblazoned with the U.S. Marines logo to collect his prize and have his photo taken for the local paper. It felt good to know someone like him won.

Then the judge announced, "In the category of largest single fish, the winner is Jake Jardinelli for a seven-pound, nine-ounce largemouth bass."

I jumped two feet off the ground and gave Babbo the biggest bear hug ever. After that, we bounced up and down together for at least ten minutes, perhaps a slight exaggeration.

FOUR

The final award for the grand prize was the only one remaining. Babbo stood in front of the crowd, next to another fisherman in worn-out overalls who was wringing his hands and rocking from one foot to the other. I recognized him as the guy I saw fishing from an old, battered kayak instead of a fishing boat. It obviously did the job, judging by his haul of fish.

The judge lifted his bullhorn to his lips and said, "The grand prize for the 20th Anniversary Firecracker Fishing Tournament goes to James Jardinelli."

Mamma threw her arms around Babbo's neck and squealed. "Oh Jimmy, you did it. You finally got your boat."

Sporting an ear-to-ear smile, Babbo rushed to the winner's table to collect his trophy. Babbo and I stood next to our new boat for photos that would appear in the local paper. "Father and son team wins big at Firecracker Fishing Tournament," would be the headline.

While a guy from the Lund's dealership got ready to hitch the boat trailer to our pickup, the kayak guy, a skinny woman, and a couple of raggedy little girls watched from the side. The youngest girl, who looked about six years old, clung to the woman's waist with one arm and wiped her eyes with the other.

"Congratulations," the kayak guy said to Babbo. "That sure is a nice boat you won there."

Babbo talked with him for a while, then came over and draped his arm across my shoulders the way he does when he has something important to say.

"That guy's name is Ron. He and his family are going through some tough times. His wife is pretty sick, and he uses the fish he catches to help feed the family. How would you feel if we let him take the boat?"

I couldn't believe what I was hearing. After finally winning the boat he'd wanted for years, Babbo was ready to give away his prized possession to someone we didn't even know. I rubbed the back of my neck while I glanced over at Ron and his family. That little kid was in the middle of a gut-wrenching sob. What could I say? It didn't seem fair to give up our prize, but it also didn't feel right to hang onto something Ron and his family needed more than we did.

"Ok, whatever you say, Babbo. Would we still get to use it?" I asked. Babbo just smiled.

Mamma talked with the woman, whose name we found out is Annie, and learned about her struggles with a chronic disease. Annie's medical expenses were enormous, and sometimes she couldn't even take care of the house or the kids. Before we left, Mamma made plans to cook some of her favorite dishes at Annie's house. Mamma also volunteered Jesse and me to help with some of the chores. I'm okay with that.

As Babbo and I loaded our gear into the truck, Jesse asked Mamma to help her fold an origami fish she got from the Brit's

Fish and Chips food truck. They did that while we drove home, which is why we were so surprised when we got there.

"Where's my car?" Mamma blurted.

As the overhead door opened to our garage, we were all surprised to see it empty.

"Did somebody steal your car from the garage?" Babbo asked.

"No, I left it at the park," Mamma giggled.

In our excitement, all four of us forgot that she drove separately to the park. So we went back to retrieve her car, laughing the entire way.

Oh yeah, I almost forgot an important thing that happened when the local Lund's dealer found out Babbo was giving away his new boat. He said anyone who would do something like that deserved a reward. His shop recently got a '93 Lund Tyee 1650 boat with a 95hp motor as a trade-in. That's the kind with a steering wheel, windshield, and four seats, enough for Mamma and Jesse to ride with us in comfort. It needed some work and it was too old for them to sell, but it was ours for free if we wanted it. Babbo burst out in a rendition of "Santa Lucia" when the dealer offered it to him.

We found out Ron was very resourceful and mechanical. He helped Babbo tune up the motor and spruce up the interior of our boat. Now it's a classic that gets attention from everyone that sees it. Sometimes Babbo, Ron, and I go fishing in his boat while Mamma and the girls cruise the shore in our boat. We do this a lot on Sundays, after we meet up at church.

This whole thing turned out to be way better than that trophy fish I was dreaming about. I guess it's true that you can never outgive God.

59

Now to him who is able to do far more abundantly than all that we ask or think, according to the power at work within us, to him be glory in the church and in Christ Jesus throughout all generations, forever and ever. Amen.

— EPHESIANS 3:20-21 (ESV)

ALL THE DEEPEST COLORS

BY KAREN INGLE

Karen Ingle writes stories from the rural southwestern Minnesota home she shares with her husband Dennis. Together, they have raised five adults and a multitude of chickens. Pass her in the aisles at Walmart, and you'll see a rather ordinary woman. But dig deeper and you'll find a lady whose life journey traversed the hills and dales of widowhood, single motherhood, adoption, and more moving than should be legal. Deeper still you'll discover a settled joy the world cannot give.

A freelance writer and author, Karen also serves as communications manager for her local pregnancy center. Her experiences there—combined with her journalistic interviews—have compelled her to launch the Rumors of Light series of Christian romantic suspense novels. The first, *With Me in the Storm*, released in 2022.

Connect with Karen Ingle at
kareningleauthor.com
On social media @kareningleauthor

ONE

If Grandpa and I ever argued, it was only about colors. Or his ancient pickup. Or both.

Bouncing home along the gravel road from town, I kept the driver's side window half open to capture some breeze, since Grandpa's AC didn't work. Over the road noise, I yelled, "That's baloney, Grandpa! This truck of yours is an oxidized robin's egg blue. Complete with little rusty spots."

"Hmph." Grandpa pursed his lips to hide his smirk. "I don't know what's wrong with your eyes, Mike. It's a deep turquoise, the same as the sky in summer. Just like today," he added, waving a gnarled finger toward the top of the windshield.

I smiled as I drove. Grandpa did too. Then he took a long chug of his grapefruit Squirt while drops of condensation dripped from his fingers.

"So," he said, belching softly. "You haven't told me how it went at the high school while I was chewing the fat with Stan at the elevator."

I shrugged. "I let them talk me into it."

He smacked my leg. "Good. Your art teacher is right. You should do a senior exhibit." He wiped his wet hand on his overalls and added, elbowing me, "Even if your eye for color isn't the best."

I shook my head. "Mom won't like it." Like she wouldn't like that I was out here driving Grandpa's decrepit pickup. "It will eat up lots of my time and energy. She really wants me to do something else with my life. Something I can earn a living at."

Grandpa looked down at his Squirt can and let out a long breath. Same kind of breath that he usually let out after being around Mom too long.

I rounded the last curve before home and slowed, pumping the old brakes to make them respond. While my feet worked, my whole head turned to let my eyes drink in the glorious sight of our apple orchard spreading uphill north of the road. Hundreds of trees, billions of leaves, at least a dozen shades of green—all rippling in the breeze sweeping the hillside.

"Ditch!" Grandpa said.

I wrenched the steering wheel to the right just as the tall grass slapped inside the wheel well. "Sorry."

Grandpa shook his head and spoke quietly, eyeing the orchard. "It takes your breath away, doesn't it?"

His trained eyes scanned the rows of trees that he and countless Richards ancestors had planted. My dad and I had put in the spindly First Kiss saplings in the fourth row. Next year, we hoped to get our hands on some of the University's new Triumph variety. But I think Grandpa saw more than the apple trees. As I watched him, I had that funny feeling he was seeing something beyond the orchard.

The truck coughed and rolled to a sleepy stop, the engine sputtering.

Grandpa turned his watery eyes on me. "Need a theme for your senior exhibit?"

I blinked. I hadn't thought that far yet. The show wouldn't be until spring, anyway, right before my graduation.

Grandpa jerked his chin toward the hillside. "There you go. Free inspiration."

That seed had barely taken root when insistent tapping hit Grandpa's window.

Mom. Blond ponytail pulled tight, standing in the south ditch, up to her knees in grass.

I wrestled the gear shift into park while Grandpa rolled his window the rest of the way down.

"Hey, Mom," I said.

"Get home. Now." Her eyes flashed past Grandpa at me. Deep frown, hands on hips; all bad news.

"Yes, ma'am," I said, the only permissible answer.

As I shifted into drive, Grandpa cleared his throat beside me. Years ago, he might have tried to step in and apologize to Mom for making me do something she didn't like. He finally gave up. Now, as I drove carefully forward so as not to spray Mom with road dust, he just shot me a sympathetic look. And I returned it. Grandpa and I were on the same team. But we still had to live at home.

He would cope by napping in his wooden chair propped against the fence in the shade of the apple trees. His hat tipped forward over his face. I would concentrate on doing everything I was told for the next several days.

Two

Grandpa was Dad's dad. Mom said apple cider ran in their veins.

I think some ran in my veins, too, though as a teenager, I sometimes needed a stern look from Dad to rev up my work ethic. Once I was out in the orchard with him, however, the work always felt good.

Dad usually couldn't wait to slough off his business casual and slip into a T-shirt and jeans after a day in the office. He'd take to the hillside whistling. Soon the V between his eyebrows would disappear as he mowed or pruned or thinned fruit buds with his fingers. He enjoyed offering whatever the orchard needed from him.

Mom tried to have as little to do with the family business as possible. So when we moved into Grandpa and Grandma's house after Grandma died, she exerted no effort to make the house her home. I once heard her tell Dad that there was no need since we'd all be moving back out and selling the orchard as soon as Grandpa died too.

That was seven years ago. And Grandpa and the orchard showed no signs of disappearing from our lives. At least, none that I noticed.

In mid-August, I trudged along the aisles of trees with Grandpa and Dad, pulling the garden cart. The two of them talked like good friends. All about vole damage, the codling moths seen at the neighbors' place, and which apple varieties would be ready first. I kept my eyes on the ground, watching for windfalls. My job was to pounce on the fallen fruit and toss it into my cart. Sweat already soaked the back of my shirt and trickled into my eyes each time I bent over. I swiped the back of my hand across my forehead and reached for my water bottle.

Dad looked back at me and stopped walking. "Pop, what say we take a break here in the shade and drink some water?"

Grandpa accepted his water bottle and eased himself down onto the grass without too much trouble. Leaning his back against the cart, he pointed his feet downhill. The shade swayed across his face, tilted upward to take a good, long drink. He lifted his seed cap and wiped his arm across his short gray hair.

I followed his gaze up into the branches overhead. Smooth red apples hung like ornaments carefully placed on all the branches.

"These'll go soon," he said. He waved his cap at me and asked me to grab him an apple. I picked three that felt right in my hand and showed mostly red.

We each sank our teeth into the crisp flesh. Mine was still on the tart side, but oh, it tasted good on a hot day. While Dad and Grandpa talked over who'd be on the picking crew this year, I let my gaze drift from tree to tree and down the hill. Grandpa's old blue truck sat at the bottom, just inside the barn-red fence that bordered the grassy ditch. Suddenly, my vision zoomed in on that image. I could use carmine for the fence, equal parts white and cerulean for the truck, chromium green for the grass....

Bingo. I had it. My senior exhibit: *Seasons in the Orchard.* In an instant, I jumped to my feet, whipped out my cell phone, and started capturing images. Close-ups of the smooth red Zestars and State Fairs where they hung ripening among leaves that flapped lime-green when backlit by the summer sun. Wide shots of the entire hillside, taken through branches and along the open aisle. I heard Dad laughing as I took my fortieth picture.

"Mike, you got a Japanese beetle up your back?" he called.

I grinned. "No, just an idea."

Grandpa shielded his eyes to peer at me. Then he put his seed cap back on and took another drink of water without saying a word.

Later that night, shadowed under the solitary light over the kitchen table, Mom and Dad fell to talking about money again. I slipped out of the living room and rapped on Grandpa's bedroom door. He stood yawning, hair on end, in his V-neck undershirt and striped pajama shorts, but he invited me in anyway.

"I'm gonna do it, Grandpa. I'm gonna paint the orchard in all its seasons for my exhibit." I showed him the pictures I'd taken.

He squinted at the photos on my phone, nodding as my half-baked ideas poured out. Then he tapped the phone screen. "You plan to paint 'em these colors?"

I took the phone back and shifted one shoulder, uneasy. "Um, well, the best I can, anyway."

"These aren't the real colors, you know. The original colors." His face was intense, holding me in place. Maybe there were nights when he wasn't quite clear-headed. But this wasn't one of them.

He tapped a knobby finger at his temple. "I remember when the colors were deeper. The apples were...more red. The grass was more green."

His eyes kept me riveted.

"And He—" he went on, wagging a finger toward the ceiling, "—He remembers when they were the deepest."

In the wake of his gentle, rumbling voice, my heart beat harder, and I drew in a long, deep breath. For a moment, caught up in Grandpa's eyes, I could almost see The Garden, the first trees. Flawless beauty. The Creator's love expressed in living color. So rich. So deep. So much of God in all that beauty. I wanted to cry.

"Now, I may not see so well," he said, bringing his rough hand down to rest on my arm. "But someday, there will be spring for me. And I will see it all as He sees it. Again."

He patted my arm. "Good night, Squirt."

THREE

Summer hurried onward, and orchard life got busy. We hired harvesters from among our neighbors—friends living in houses tucked into groves we could barely see from our house. They drove over daily to don white cotton gloves and drop-bottom baskets hung at their waists. They picked like champs, right alongside Dad and me. From the lower-grade "#2" apples that he sorted from our harvest, Grandpa made cider with his barrel-shaped wooden press. Younger neighbor kids helped him crank the press and bottle the juice. They always went home with a sticky quart jug of cider and sometimes a bottle of last year's natural cider vinegar if they had sickness in the family. The rest went into our orchard store. Mom handled the sales, putting on a friendly smile for all the customers. The busy season had begun.

Sometimes I'd pick all day until I could barely lift my paintbrush after supper. But the early evening light was too good to miss. So, ignoring my complaining muscles, I would lay my easel, a canvas, and my paints in the garden cart and drag the whole deal to the north side of the road. Just inside the fence, I would sit watching Grandpa snooze in his chair, with the pale blue pickup lounging in the grass like an old dog, waiting to be taken for a ride again.

Painting came easier out there. My shoulders would stop aching. And so would my heart. The colors would dance off my palette and onto the canvas, with my brush for their choreographer.

After a half-hour or so, Grandpa would snort himself awake, tip his chair back up, and amble over to see what I had painted. I'd lift my eyebrows and wait to see his expression. He'd peer from the orchard to my canvas, nod, and usually say, "The colors should be deeper."

Around the first of September, I tried taking his advice. Just on one of the smaller canvases, one I didn't mind tossing if it went wrong. But it didn't. I feared it would be a caricature of nature, an airbrushed version of reality. Instead, the image seemed to come alive. I could almost taste the halved apple, feel the juice trickle down my chin, hear the bee buzzing nearby. The next day, I deepened the colors on two more paintings. Grandpa stopped commenting. He'd just smile, scratch his stubbly cheek, and amble back to the house.

When I stood the paintings in the corner of my room to dry, I'd leave the curtains above my bed open to let the late-summer twilight caress the colors. It was a silent conversation between me and my Creator. And I'd feel like He was pleased for now.

With my senior year bulldozing toward me, I couldn't help wishing.... If only art were "the good works God had created me to do," like our pastor preached about. But Mom was sure

God had something else in mind. Something that involved burying myself in textbooks for years, then finding myself an office from which I could bring home a paycheck at least as big as Dad's.

Someone once asked me why I prefer the word "autumn" over "fall."

It's because of that September.

Every day after school, all my friends who didn't play football rode their bikes out to the orchard to join the harvesting crew. We'd already picked Zestars and State Fairs together. So they knew the system: learn how each variety looked when ripe, grip the apples near the stem, pop them loose and place them in your picking basket, gently dump your picking basket into a crate, and haul that crate to Dad's white pickup for final sorting. We might do a little "whooping and hollering," as Grandpa called it, but we picked our fair share of apples. The guys all got paid. I got to live at home.

We were part way through the McIntoshes when the accident happened. The adult morning crew was still clearing out late Estevals down on the far side of the hill. But the McIntosh trees were a significant distance away, uphill to the west. So when my crew and I arrived from school, Dad drove Grandpa's pickup, coughing and wheezing its way up the hill to our aisle, loaded with gloves and baskets, crates, and two ladders. He passed out peanut butter and jelly sandwiches, chips, and water, which we gratefully wolfed down. Then we suited up for work.

Dad and I each grabbed a ladder and set them up beside

trees in parallel rows. I took the uphill row. To this day, I wish I had picked the downhill one. Grandpa shouted, "Go!" and the race was on.

Despite the late-season heat and humidity, Dad's group and mine enjoyed heckling each other. With each crate a group lugged to the old pickup, Grandpa, perched on the tailgate in his overalls, hollered out their "score." Then he sorted the #2's into bushel baskets and stacked the crates in the truck's bed.

Five trees down my row, my group lagged way behind Dad's. "Hey, slowpoke," he shouted as he placed his three-legged ladder among the branches of his ninth tree.

From my perch, I could see the old blue truck already held dozens of full crates and a bushel or two of #2's. "Dad," I called out, "don't you think you should unload the truck down at the shed?"

"Hah!" Dad laughed. "And let you catch up? I'm not falling for that one!" He climbed the ladder and resumed picking.

When I hurried to move my own ladder to my sixth tree, I got it tangled up in a branch bowed down with apples.

"Whoa! Watch that fruit," Grandpa called out and slid off the tailgate to give me a hand.

Just as Grandpa reached me, something metallic popped, drawing our eyes to the pickup. Grandpa's ruddy face bleached white.

The old blue pickup rolled backward, away from us along the grassy aisle. Gravity tugged it downhill toward Dad's row. My friends on the ground scattered. For a blurred moment, I couldn't think, couldn't move. The truck rattled and bounced, accelerating downhill.

Then I saw Dad on his ladder, eyes wide over the roof of the runaway pickup. In the next awful second, the truck and ladder collided. Dad fell, spinning off the ladder. His back and head making a sickening crunch against the rim of the truck bed. The truck barreled on until it smashed into another tree. But Dad lay still on the olive-green grass, spilling pyrrole red blood into the black orchard soil.

FOUR

Dad's coma lasted several weeks.

For the first few days, I stayed with Mom at Aunt Irene's house in the Cities, near the hospital. In my memory, that week is one long blank, a white chunk of nothingness in the middle of what had always been—for seven years—our most colorful season of all.

Dad's brother, Irene's husband, Steve, stayed with Grandpa to keep him and the orchard operating. Without Dad's salary, the orchard store would be our main source of income until... whatever happened.

After about a week, Mom insisted that I get back to school. I suppose she felt one person staring at Dad all day was sufficient. So, Aunt Irene drove me home on a Sunday afternoon, stopping for groceries on the way. When we neared the house, the orchard rose on my right. The picking crew was into the Cortlands and Honeycrisps now. Bordering the apple trees, the grove radiated warm autumn colors. But something looked different.

"Where's Grandpa's old truck?" I asked, watching its empty spot beside the fence slide past my window.

Aunt Irene pulled up to the mailbox at the end of our driveway. "Your Grandpa had it towed away," she said. She reached her long, manicured fingers into the box and pulled out handful after handful of mail, heaping it on the seat between us. Then she looked at me. "You okay?"

I turned my face to the window. I felt like my favorite dog had just been put to sleep.

She seemed to hear what I didn't say. After a pause, she said, "Right. Let's go see what Grandpa's up to, hey?"

Grandpa should have been in the pressing room. But the press stood idle, a faint vinegar scent mingling with the usual sweetness in the air. Behind me, one of my friends knocked on the door frame. "Hey, Mike. Saw you drive up. Came to say— Good to see you."

"You, too." We both shoved our hands in our pockets and stared at the motionless cider press. Finally, I asked, "You know where my grandpa is?"

He nodded, tipping his head toward the orchard. "Picking, picking, and picking some more. C'mon, I'll walk up with you."

We didn't talk. But it was good to have someone there, climbing the hill beside me. When he pointed, I could see Grandpa's arms reaching up inside a tree, picking fast, like his life depended on it.

"He's a harvesting machine, your grandfather. It's like he's trying to do both your work and your dad's."

Uncle Steve dismounted his ladder and crossed the aisle to say something to his dad. Grandpa just shook his head and went on picking apples. He topped out his crate and carried it to Dad's white pickup, where another friend of mine sat on the bed sorting out the #2's.

I watched for a few minutes, then turned to go. My friend said something, but I didn't answer. Everything just felt wrong at the moment. Maybe it always would.

Aunt Irene made a huge supper for the four of us. Uncle Steve and Grandpa gave me good, strong hugs when they came to the table, all damp and smelling of Kirk's Castille Soap. Irene passed around the chicken and the potatoes and the one update she'd heard from Mom: nothing had changed.

Grandpa, his eyelids drooping, looked about ten years older than he'd been last week. He hadn't shaved, and his stiff gray hair stuck out over his ears. He said little and left the table after eating one polite helping of everything.

When Aunt Irene waved away my offer of help with the dishes, I thought I might just go say hi to him. But at Grandpa's door, I could hear him inside, sobbing.

Not knowing what to do with that, I went to bed and lay for hours, staring at the blank ceiling.

In late October, Dad came home in a wheelchair. Uncle Steve helped him transfer from the car, and Grandpa and I lined up along the front walk. As Mom wheeled him from the car to the front door, Dad lifted his hand when he reached me. I took it and squeezed. He didn't squeeze back. He looked at me quizzically, like I might need to re-introduce myself. But when he murmured, "Hi, Mike," my throat closed up, and my eyes watered.

He lifted his hand to Grandpa, too, and murmured, "Pop."

But Mom hurried him into the house. Grandpa scratched the back of his neck and put his seed cap back on.

"C'mon, Mike," he said, turning toward the orchard. "All we have left are Keepsakes."

I paused for a moment at the look in his eyes.

"Yep, just Keepsakes now," he muttered, reaching for the cotton gloves hanging halfway out of his back pocket. He took a few steps, stumbled, and recovered. "Almost done, Squirt."

I zipped up my heavy sweatshirt, flipped up the hood, pulled on my gloves. Side by side, Grandpa and I trudged up the drive, silent with our thoughts. Would Dad be back in the orchard next autumn? Or would we again need to hire help to press the cider, make the pies, and man the store? Or would Mom just sell everything and move us into town?

At the end of the driveway, Grandpa suddenly listed to his right. He leaned against the mailbox, then slumped to the ground.

"Grandpa! Grandpa, what's wrong?" I knelt and lifted his head onto my lap. "Can you hear me, Grandpa?"

The left side of Grandpa's mouth moved, but the sounds made no sense. His eyes didn't quite focus on me, and everything right of his nose sagged toward his jaw.

I yanked off my gloves, dug out my cell phone, and dialed 911.

FIVE

As more December snow settled on the orchard across the road, I watched through my bedroom window. Despite the clouds, sunrise cast a faint pink tint across the hillside. I snapped another picture of the orchard, just out of habit. It was all sharp bare branches and soft pillows of snow now. Two or three browns, at least four shades of white.

I layered a plaid flannel shirt over my long-sleeved T-shirt and headed toward Mom and Dad's room. Like the falling snow, we were settling in, too. Each weekday, Mom and I helped Dad get up and dressed and fed. Then Mrs. Halvorson, a retired nurse, came to spend the day with him. Mom drove me to school on her way to work at the market. After school, I walked the two blocks to Grandpa's nursing home, where they let me paint in his room until Mom came to get me.

Eventually, I knew I'd have to get a paying job too. For now, however, Mom let me paint beside Grandpa. She said it was because I had that senior exhibit coming. But maybe she had other reasons.

That day, on the drive to school, I got a good look at my mom. Her blond hair seemed grayer than I remembered it being. She steered with one hand, and with the other, tucked her hair behind her ear. When she reached for her thermal mug of coffee, it occurred to me that it was a new habit.

"Mom," I began, knowing this conversational ice was thin, "how are you doing?"

She turned her head to look at me. Then she turned back to the road. "You've never asked me that before, Mike."

"I—I'm sorry. I should have."

She swallowed. Minutes passed. "I'm tired. I'm worried. It's your senior year, and...things are just so...out of control." Suddenly she was bawling, right there on the seat next to me. She hit the brakes and just stopped in the middle of the road. I reached across and shifted into park.

"Here, Mom," I said and opened my arms. She tipped toward me and just cried and cried and cried.

Nobody used this road in the winter but us. It was just me and Mom and the snow. The snowflakes fell silently while Mom sobbed into the one tissue I found for her in the glove compartment.

Mom quit crying about the time the snow let up. "Sorry, Mike," she said, blotting her eyes with the shreds of her tissue.

"I guess you needed to let it out."

She nodded, drawing the back of her hand under her nose. "It's been tough. Oh, for heaven's sake—" She gestured at the digital clock. "You'll be late for school."

Mom set the truck rolling again. She nudged her wavy hair away from her face as she drove, checking her makeup in the rearview mirror. "What a mess."

I sat back, studying her. An unfamiliar warmth rose in my chest. "Mom, I think you're beautiful."

She cry-laughed or hiccupped or something. But she smiled just a little, too.

When our pickup crunched to the icy curbside in front of my high school, I climbed out with my backpack. Mom leaned over to say, "Thanks, Mike. And, hey, when you see Grandpa today, please tell him I said hi."

"Sure, Mom. Or you can come in," I added.

The second smile of the day crossed her lips. "Yeah. Maybe I will."

That afternoon, Grandpa was extra sleepy. To get the best light, I usually sat with my easel to his right, between me and the door. Unfortunately, that put Grandpa behind me, so I would occasionally turn and look at him in case he tried to tell me something.

Gone was his rumbling voice, his throaty chuckle. He mumbled now, if he said anything at all.

Around four-thirty, I stretched, put down my brush, and stood up to get a fresh look at my painting from across the room. Grandpa's still form made hills and valleys in the snowy white blanket that covered him. Beyond his bed stood the painting I had dubbed *Winter Covers the Orchard*: a snowy hill yet to be punctuated by the trees I would add next.

Grandpa. Orchard. It was winter for Grandpa's body. Was he lying there, cloaked in white, his true self silent and submerged, just waiting for spring?

A knock sounded at the door. Our new pastor, who liked us to call him Mark, peeked around it. "Mind if I come in?" he asked.

"Not at all." I moved my easel so he could get to the one chair in the room.

"How's your grandpa today?" He moved closer to the bed, watching Grandpa sleep.

I shrugged. "He's been asleep most of the afternoon. We don't usually talk much."

When Mark faced me, he noticed my painting and the photo clipped to the easel. "Your orchard, I take it?"

"Yep." I tried to see it as Mark might, but I could only picture what I was going to make of it. There would be twiggy trees, bluish shadows, and a graying sky like I'd seen yesterday.

He pulled a pocket New Testament out from inside his wool coat. "Mike, there was a passage going through my head as I walked over today. Is it okay if I read that to you?"

"Sure." I sat on the corner of Grandpa's bed. He grunted and shifted slightly.

"It's from Romans 8, verses 20-23." Mark turned a few pages. As he started reading, Grandpa stirred on his bed.

"Grandpa," I said, patting his leg, "Pastor Mark is here. Can you hear him?"

More grunts.

As Mark read, one of Grandpa's eyes opened halfway, then the other. He was listening.

"'...in hope that the creation itself also will be set free from its slavery to corruption into the freedom of the glory of the children of God...'"

Grandpa tried to say something.

Mark paused, looking from Grandpa to me with raised eyebrows. I didn't understand any more than Mark did.

Grandpa fell silent, and Mark resumed reading. "'And not only that but also we ourselves, having the first fruits of the

Spirit, even we ourselves groan within ourselves, waiting eagerly for our adoption as sons, the redemption of our body.'"

"Yaaah..." Grandpa said. His face took on that intense, focused look he sometimes wore. But he wasn't focused on Mark or me. He faced the window and tried to sit up.

Mark set down his Bible and reached to support Grandpa. "Walter? What is it you'd like to say, Walter?"

Grandpa's watery eyes turned toward Mark, and he grabbed the pastor's arm. His mouth moved, but nothing came out. Then he spotted me.

"Myyyyg," he said, arm extending toward me. "Ssssprehng." His arm swung toward the window, his gnarled finger pointing at something only he could see.

He repeated it. "Ssssprehng. Myyyyg, luuuuk!"

I ran to the window. My face, my hands pressed against the glass. "What is it, Grandpa? What does it look like?"

He didn't answer.

Mark spoke quietly. "Mike."

I whirled. Grandpa was gone. His body lay slack in Mark's arms.

For a moment, I couldn't move. It had happened. Just like that. I walked to the bed and picked up one of Grandpa's rough hands. Tears trickled down my cheeks.

Mark gently closed Grandpa's eyelids.

It must have been then I realized Grandpa was now seeing all the deepest colors.

SIX

Other families' funerals always made me feel awkward. So I was surprised at how many of my friends came to Grandpa's visitation. I stood out in the funeral home lobby with them, most of us silent, just grateful for friendship in a tough time.

"Your Grandpa was a great guy, Mike," one friend said.

"He always remembered to ask about my little sister," another added. "His vinegar made her feel better, too."

"I'm really sorry, Mike. I know you're going to miss him." A pat on the shoulder, a couple of sniffles, and we all got quiet again.

My mom took my elbow from behind. "Excuse me, Mike. Mark's wife would like to talk to you for a moment."

I nodded to my friends and walked back to the little chapel with Mom. She clung to the crook of my arm. She'd been doing that a lot the last few days.

Dad had asked the funeral director to display my four largest paintings—one of each season in the orchard—near the foot of Grandpa's casket. Almost like he wanted Grandpa to be able to look at them while he napped there. All that was missing was his hat tipped down over his eyes.

Dad sat in his wheelchair between Mark and Mark's wife Sophia, pointing out the old blue truck parked along the fence in *Summer Serenity*. My favorite of the four. I swallowed and blinked hard.

Mark turned and shook my hand. "Mike. Holding up okay?"

I nodded half-heartedly, then shook hands with his wife.

Sophia gave me a soft smile. "Mark tells me these paintings are all yours. They're...Well, they're exquisite." She moved closer to the last one I'd done, completely from memory. *Spring Comes to the Orchard* had sort of flown onto the canvas in the two days after Grandpa died. Leaning in, she said, "I notice this one is somewhat unique among the collection, in that you applied fewer layers of paint."

I pulled in a breath. "Do you paint?"

A crooked smile tugged at the corner of her mouth, and she glanced at Mark. "You might say so. I'd love to hear how this group of pieces came about."

I turned back to the summer painting, feeling myself drawn into the damp heat and the whining cicadas and the brightness. I could hear Grandpa's voice: *The colors should be deeper.* I described Grandpa's gift for seeing things as God intended them to be, not just as they were. The way I could see my paintings, finished before all the strokes were in place.

Just as I began to feel a little foolish for rambling on like I was, Sophia reached into her purse, first for a tissue to wipe her eyes. Then for a business card, which she handed to me.

"Mike, this isn't the best time, I know. But when things quiet down, let's talk. About art school, and scholarships." She gestured toward the card in my hand, which bore the X-shaped logo of the Minnesota College of Art and Design. "I'm just an adjunct right now, but I know talent like yours is what the school is looking for."

I stole a glance at Mom beside me. She squeezed my elbow, and I relaxed. Her eyes welled up as she whispered, "Wouldn't your grandpa be proud?"

Dad, grinning, rolled himself close and patted my lower back. I leaned down to wrap an arm around his shoulders. From there, I could read my signature on *Spring Comes to the Orchard,* just past the edge of Grandpa's casket: Mike "Squirt" Richards.

A Finch in Time

by Liz Kimmel

LIZ KIMMEL is a poet at heart and creator of supplemental educational resources. She writes for several Guideposts publications, and is included in all of the Short and Sweet books by Grace Publishing to date.

These are collections of stories using words of just one syllable (with a few exceptions). Her most recent book, available by early 2023, is an alliterative retelling of several of the parables of Jesus. Liz spent twenty years working in Medical Records at a local hospital, two years in Trust Operations at Well Fargo Bank, and twenty years in the front office of her church, Bethel Christian Fellowship. She loves her busy life as a retiree. In addition to writing, Liz provides admin support for three nonprofits (Great Commission Media Ministries, Dare to Believe Ministries, and the Minnesota Christian Writers Guild).

She and her husband of forty-three years have two children and four delightful grandchildren.

Website: lizkimmelwordwright.com/

ONE
THE ONSET OF SPRING

Two best friends perched near each other in their favorite birch tree and had a terrific view of the entire community. The buds were just poking their way out of the ends of the branches, but there were no leaves restricting their line of sight yet. Fin balanced effortlessly on the slender branch, while Woody seemed like he was standing vertically on the tree's trunk. There were so many things different about them. Fin had slender feet, a short beak, and a slightly rounded figure. Woody's feet were solid, his beak long, and his shape was more angular. Fin's bright yellow feathers and Woody's black and white ones contrasted sharply with each other, much as their personalities did. As dissimilar as they were, they knew that Maker had designed them both. And though an unlikely duo, they had been comrades since shortly after leaving their nests last year.

They gazed contentedly down at Mr. and Mrs. Krueger's beautiful garden. Fin and Woody loved the gardener's yard, filled with birdbaths and bird feeders and more flowers and lovely trees than a bird could hope to imagine. The Kruegers were honorary grandparents to every kid (and every bird) on the block. They didn't have any children of their own, but took it upon themselves to make their yard a special, welcoming place for everybody. The feathered friends loved to spend time both in and above their garden.

It was pretty common to see rows of sparrows or ravens lined up on a long segment of power line that stretched over them. That was a great place to hang out and discuss all the goings-on in the neighborhood. But Fin and Woody had staked out this birch tree for their very own. Their friendship was atypical. They'd been coming to this spot to tweet and chirp about many things for as long as they could remember.

A dip in the fountain below was just the thing they needed as they stretched and preened, trying to get all their feathers back in the right places after a night's sleep in the nearby trees. Fin, which was short for his family name of *Finch*, roosted in a nearby willow, but Woody preferred being tucked into the cavity of one of the pine trees. He liked holes (his beak was perfect for making them), and he wanted the safe feeling he got as he squeezed into a crevice at night to dream until the sun (or his hunger) woke him up.

A sip of water refreshed them, and they flitted back up to their observation post in the tree.. From their position high above the ground, they could see their friends returning from the south.

Spring had finally arrived. The geese flew back into town in their neat V-shaped formations and honked loudly at each other. Pretty soon the robins were there, along with the warblers and the red-winged blackbirds. It was great to see them all again after so many months apart. The potential for snow still existed, but there was a lot of melting going on. The warming weather invited the trees to bud. Green was showing up everywhere - except on the slow-pokey catalpa tree.

"I've been worried about the catalpa," Fin chirped to his friend as they studied the bare branches not far from their perch. "The other trees are all starting to get green, but I see nothing happening on her branches. Do you think she died over the winter?"

"Nah! She's just a late bloomer. That's what my folks told me when I asked them the exact same thing," responded Woody, proud of the fact that he knew something that Fin didn't know.

"Well, I sure hope she hurries up. I enjoyed sitting in the shade of her big leaves. I'd hate to think that something had happened to her." Fin recalled one of the sweltering summer days last year, when it was so unbearable as he sat on the wire with the sparrows, that he just had to find some place to cool off. He watched one of the neighborhood girls gather up the catalpa's leaves and use them to trace huge heart shapes all over the sidewalk with her chalk. While she played under the branches of the tree, Fin thought about how cool and comfortable and protected she was from the hot sun. Without hesitation, he had flown down from the wire to find a nice, shady spot high in the tree's crown. Oh, that was a nice memory.

Woody was getting impatient with Fin's reminiscing. He loved to be in motion. He needed to be in motion, especially when he was hungry. The restless woodpecker swooped over to another tree, and his vivid red head started its rhythmic beating. He had been taking a quick break from his fatherly duties to check in with Fin. Several weeks ago, as winter was waning, Woody had met the bird of his dreams, and they'd built a nest to prepare for their new family. He and Becky took turns keeping the eggs protected until they hatched, which would be any day now. Woody would have to work double-time to find enough food for everyone. He was tired just thinking about it.

He paid little attention as Fin released his grip on the branch, raised his wings, and disappeared into a ray of bright sunshine. Since Woody wasn't going to stick around and tweet with him, Fin went in search of some of their other friends. He was so curious about the adventures of Robin and Blue. Did they get tired as they flew back home from their warm winter vacation spots? How long did it take them to get here? Did the local birds along the way share their trees with the travelers? Was the food any different? Unlike people, Fin and his friends did not need maps or a GPS to know which way to go. Traveling back and forth when the seasons changed was just something they knew how to do. Maker had given all the birds that ability. But Maker also ensured Fin and Woody had everything they needed to stay safe and healthy while remaining in Minnesota year-round.

The one thing Fin really wished right now was that the catalpa tree would start to bud. He didn't want to worry about her, but as far as he could tell, she was way behind schedule. She had a bunch of catching up to do to keep pace with all the other trees in town.

While Fin was flitting around the neighborhood, he happened upon another of his favorites, the very-gated maple. At least that's what he thought Mr. Krueger was calling it. The word is *variegated*. It means something with different colors (Fin found this out from listening more closely when the gardener explained it to one of the kids). Fin wasn't variegated exactly, but he had different colors. He was so proud of his bright yellow feathers. They stood out clearly against his black forehead and wings and the little patches of white that peeked out around his tail. Maybe that's why he likes this tree so much. They were both so colorful, at least for part of the year.

He loved the leaves on this special maple tree. Each one had a creamy white border surrounding a green center. The contrast made the leaves easy to spot from a long way away. The unusual pattern had something to do with white cells not producing enough "color-fill" (or *chlorophyll*, which is the word that the gardener was actually saying). Mr. Krueger was constantly examining the branches and the leaves. If there was no white on a leaf, he had to cut off the entire stem to keep the rest of the leaves from turning to a solid color. It was a lot of work, and Fin enjoyed watching how tirelessly the gardener took care of this wonderful, beautiful tree.

Fin had a very sentimental attachment to this particular maple. This was where Fin's parents built a nest just last year, and this is where Fin hatched. His mother had laid six eggs, and after they hatched, all of them stayed in the nest for two weeks. It was the best two weeks of Fin's life. His mom and dad took such good care of them all. And when Mom laid some more eggs, they built another nest nearby. His dad was responsible for training and taking care of all the chicks. He was glad that most of his hatch-mates had stayed in town. As if anyone would want to leave the Kruegers' garden, anyway!

Two

THE SWEET DAYS OF SUMMER

Several weeks later, Fin caught up with Woody again when they just happened to settle at the same time in the same birch branches, overlooking the same catalpa tree, which now displayed unmistakable life. She had leaves! And the most beautiful flowers had appeared. Filling the tree were huge blossoms that reminded Fin of the trumpet that one of the neighbor boys played. His trumpet was pretty loud, and Fin liked to listen to the boy through the bedroom window as he practiced. It was made of shiny brass, but the catalpa's trumpet-shaped flowers were a lovely white with yellow stripes and purple speckles inside.

"What do you think of those flowers, Fin? I think they look yummy enough to eat!" chatted Woody.

"Don't be silly, Woody," chirped Fin. "You know you are much happier eating all the bugs and beetles you find hiding in the wood."

"Yeah, catalpa's flowers are pretty all right, but if I was going to have a dessert, I think I'd rather have some crabapples from Mr. Krueger's trees! Too bad I have to wait until the fall for that treat."

"Hey Woody, have you noticed all the bees that have been hovering so close to catalpa? They sure seem to pay her a lot of attention." Fin knew why the bees were there, but he just wanted to take Woody's mind off of his own stomach for a few minutes.

Woody was excited to display some more of his collected knowledge (gleaned from overhearing the gardener instructing the children). "The bees gather all the pollen from inside those blooms and carry it over to the other trees. Then they bring the nectar back to their hives and use it to make honey. That reminds me...I'm kind of hungry. I'll see you later. Gotta go find some bugs!"

Fin laughed as his friend made a hasty retreat. And soon, he heard the rhythmic tap-tap-tapping of Woody's beak against the nearest tree trunk.

Summer in Minnesota was quite a contradiction; for some, it was too hot, and for others, it was too wet. Others thought it was too buggy (not the birds, of course, because they love the bugs), and almost everybody felt like it was too short! Fin loved the summer. All his friends were around, and the sun was so lovely and bright. But this was the time of year, as all Minnesota birds knew well, when summer storms gathered in an instant and caused damage that created significant problems.

While enjoying the company of some of his chickadee friends up on the power line, Fin became aware that the wire was swaying. The wind picked up, and after glancing at the sky, Fin saw the dark and menacing clouds. He and his friends needed to find shelter fast. The chickadees made a run for the hedge near the gardener's brick wall. Fin shot for one of Mr. Krueger's birdhouses, close to his maple tree. If he didn't get there before the heavy rain started, he knew he was in big trouble. It was really hard to fly in the rain.

Fortunately, Fin made it to safety just as the sheets of rain slashed through the air and the wind blew everything in a straight line. As soon as he got inside, he realized he was not alone. Goldie scooted over to make room for him. She was the cutest little goldfinch he'd ever seen. And she had been hanging around the power line a lot lately. He tried to make himself look brave by puffing out his chest – though there wasn't much room for showing off in the tiny house. He warbled a little song that he hoped was comforting to her. Then he closed his eyes, tucked his head under his wing, and waited. And waited. And waited. It seemed like forever before the storm passed, and he could peek out from their hiding place.

He was so happy to see that his sturdy maple tree weathered the storm well. He knew that some birds had already built nests. He hoped that they could protect their eggs from the blowing winds and the pouring rain. Would Goldie be interested in building a nest with him? That was something he'd have to explore in the very near future.

He was not so happy, though, when he ventured a little farther and laid eyes on the catalpa. She had broken branches all over the ground, and many of her leaves were torn to shreds. Both Kruegers and several kids were already moving around the yard, picking up twigs that had fallen and sweeping up the torn pieces. He saw the man gently touch the catalpa's trunk as if to say, "I'm so sorry. I'll do what I can to help."

THREE

The Arrival of Autumn

Fin knew that autumn was here. He remembered it from last year. He was both excited and sad about the changes that were coming. Over the summer, he joined Woody in the fatherhood club. Goldie had said yes! The two of them spent the summer preparing for and then taking care of their new chicks. All of their babies were out on their own now, figuring out the lay of the land for themselves. They investigated every inch of the Kruegers' garden and were so excited to find the seeds and suet that Mrs. K left out for them. They especially liked the suet when she mixed it with some yummy peanut butter.

"Hey, Woody! Aren't these leaves beautiful?" Fin found his friend nestled in their birch tree and was happy to spend some time catching up with him.

Woody seemed sad. "Yeah, they're pretty. But Fin, I can't quite figure out why so many of our friends are moving away again. Why would they want to leave this lovely state? The food selection is excellent, and the neighborhood is such a great place to live. What do those other places down south have that Minnesota doesn't?"

"Well, for starters, some of them are not quite as durable as you and I are. I think they need to go to a place where the weather doesn't go below zero and snow doesn't cover all the trees and bushes. And as you well know, there's hardly enough food around here for all of us in the winter."

Woody thought about this for a few minutes and then said, "You're probably right. But I'm really gonna miss those hummingbirds. They are so tiny and so talented. I could watch them every day and not get tired of it."

Fin knew what he meant. He wished that he had the strength and stamina of the little mini-birds that loved the catalpa tree as much as he and the bees did. He wondered what it would feel like to hover in the air like they do, gathering nectar from the flowers while suspended in the air. He wanted to try it but was afraid he would collapse from the weight of his body. How can they move their wings so fast? What would it be like to fly backwards? How will they be able to fly so far away? He knew that Maker gave different abilities to different birds.. That Maker was a pretty amazing guy!

"Hey Fin, have you noticed any woolly bear caterpillars yet? The ones I've seen so far this year are almost all black. Not much of a stripe on their backs at all. You know what that means!"

"Yeah, I listened to the gardener explaining it to one of the girls. The bigger the stripe, the milder the winter would be. He isn't quite sure if it means anything or not, scientifically, that is. But if the legend is true, then we are in for some pretty severe weather this winter!" To be honest, Fin was a little concerned.

He knew how hard it was when it was soooo cold and soooo snowy aaaaaall the time for the whooooole winter.

"Well," said Woody, "I think I will just enjoy the pretty sights right now and not worry about what might or might not happen in three months. Have you noticed? The acorns are falling. I've gotta go beat those squirrels to the punch. They grab up so many of them, and then I'm left settling for the scraps. See you later!"

After Woody flew off in search of his next meal, Fin took a neighborhood tour. He was thrilled when he passed over a cluster of bright red maple trees. And right nearby were several huge oaks with brilliant yellow leaves, almost as pretty as his feathers. Although, if he were honest about it, even as the leaves were starting to get more vibrant, his bright yellow feathers were beginning to fade. This happened to him last fall, too. His beautiful yellow changed to a plain, drab brown. Thank Maker that they didn't all fall out at once! He'd never be able to fly if they did. And the one good thing about his new feathers is that they were puffier and would help keep him warm this winter. He knew that his lovely yellow feathers would come back again in the spring. Something to look forward to for sure!

He ignored his sadness about the feathers and tried not to feel too proud of his beautiful color. He had to admit that the mix of orange and green and yellow and red in all the trees was something only an artist like Maker could produce. He would never get tired of looking at them.

The interesting tamarack tree attracted his attention. He loved it because it, too, changed its colors to a beautiful golden shade. Most of the pines around town stayed green all year long, and they kept their needles. But tamarack was like some of his other favorites. It changed its appearance as the weather cooled, and it dropped its needles like the maple and catalpa trees did. In fact, most of the trees around the neighborhood were losing their leaves now. There were birch trees and aspen, ash and cottonwood, cedar, spruce, cherry.... He could go on and on. How in the world did Maker come up with so many great ideas? He was definitely the Master when it came to design!

Fin was glad to see that not all of his friends left town when the temperatures began to drop. Thankfully, his finch family stayed nearby. The sparrows were friendly and such good company, and his little buddies, the chickadees, never had a bad tweet to say about anybody. And while the cardinals and blue jays were not quite as neighborly, they were beautiful to look at. Then there were the neighborhood bullies, who always stuck around. Fin kind of wished the crows would have been the ones to migrate south for the winter. He was sometimes a little scared of them. They were so big and so bossy. If they saw something they wanted, Fin had better not interfere!

FOUR
THE WONDER OF WINTER

As the days passed, it appeared that the woolly bear caterpillar was right again. Temperatures dipped lower and lower while the snow piled higher and higher. Where did it all come from? How could it possibly get any deeper? And if the sun was still shining in the sky (which it was), why was it so freezing cold? These were all questions he hoped to ask Maker when he had the chance.

One of the coolest things about this season of the year was the fact that most of the trees were now completely bare. Fin just loved to sit on the wire and study them. Most of his friends didn't want to join him when it was so cold out. But he had noticed that there was just the tiniest bit of warmth coursing through the wire – just enough to keep it from freezing. It felt good on his feet. The owls liked to sit on the poles nearby and keep an eye on the neighborhood. But Fin had to stay up late or get up early if he would see any of them.

As he perched above the Kruegers' garden, he let his eyes take in all of his well-known trees. It was amazing to see them without their leaves. He knew what they felt like (given his feather situation). He could see every trunk, every branch, and every twig. It was incredible how differently they were formed. The birch trees were so tall, and their arms stretched straight up to the sky. The graceful willow trees had branches that hung low toward the ground, almost as if they wanted to touch the rabbits and squirrels that scurried around. His dear friend catalpa had so many curves and bends; he couldn't imagine what had happened to cause them to grow so crooked. And the massive oak trees spread their arms wide out to the sides, encompassing everyone and everything in their reach.

As Fin looked more closely at the oak trees, he noticed that some had kept their leaves throughout the winter. He realized *that* was the sound he heard as he flew nearby, the sound of leaves rustling in the wind. It was a sound that seemed out of place against the white backdrop of winter.

Woody settled in the tree next to him. He had also been wondering about the oaks. "Fin, why do you think the oak leaves didn't fall like the leaves on all the other trees?" This was one thing that he had never heard Mr. or Mrs. Krueger discussing with the kids, and he wanted to know the answer.

Fin's eyes brightened as he realized that he thought of the oaks as the grandparents of all the other trees. He imagined they were clapping their hands for Maker, just like the children did when they were happy about something.

"You know, Woody, it seems like they are determined to use their strength to honor Maker. And they won't let the wind take their leaves until they are good and ready to release them. The only thing that's going to make that happen is when the new little buds push their way out in a couple of months."

Woody bobbed his head in agreement. "I think you're onto

something, Fin. And all of this deep thinking has left me mighty hungry. I'm going to see if I can find some undiscovered fruit hanging on any of the bushes nearby. But if not, I did happen to notice that Mrs. Krueger put out some good-looking seeds in her bird feeder. Hopefully the Jays haven't eaten them all. See you later!"

Fin tweeted a goodbye and sat quietly on the branch for a while longer, letting his eyes roam over the whole neighborhood. He saw the Kruegers' garden and was so thankful for all the ways they took care of this corner of the world. He saw his beloved variegated maple tree, where he had entered the world and where his chicks had done the same. He saw the oaks, steadfastly hanging on to what remained of the past, even as the new season was being birthed deep inside the tips of each branch. He saw the willows and the tamarack and all the other variations of magnificent trees that provided food and shelter for so many of Fin's friends. Maker sure did have a wonderful way of taking care of His creation from one season to the next.

And then he looked down, and his eyes rested on the lovely catalpa tree. Her flowers had faded a long time ago, and her leaves had all been raked up. But the long, skinny seed pods remained, dangling from the branches like ornaments on the Kruegers' Christmas tree. Fin knew from watching the pods last year that they would stay intact until the spring arrived. When they finally opened, the wind would catch their winged seeds and scatter them as far as it could carry them.

Maybe that's another reason why Fin loved the catalpa tree so much. At its very core, it could fly. Just like Fin.

The Father Sees

by Marianne McDonough

Marianne McDonough, a journalist from Edina, Minnesota, loves to study people, history, animals, the intricacies of language, the wonders of the universe, and most of all, the One Who set it all in motion. A two-time cancer survivor, she has authored two books about empowerment in the cancer journey. This short story is her first offering in published fiction.

Marianne believes in the power of prayer, because that's how life works best. She doesn't measure success by projects, money, or position. Instead, she focuses on virtuous character and seeks to convey that fundamental value in her writing. She believes that our omniscient God is the One Whose approval most counts. Excellence in attitude, kindness, and integrity, she says, comprise true success and lasting legacies.

Thus, she hopes *"The Father Sees"* story will encourage readers to seek God's approval above all else and live their lives for His glory.

Learn more about Marianne on her website:

www.mariannemcdonough.com

www.8stepstogettingrealwithcancer.com

www.beatingcanceronetruthatatime.com

ONE

6:05 p.m., Wednesday, August 1, 2007

A normal evening commute on a Minneapolis bridge almost took Megan Winfield's life. As she sat in bumper-to-bumper traffic on the Hennepin Avenue Bridge, she heard a loud boom, and the bridge shifted laterally. Then, a few seconds later, a thunderous snap of steel cracked and buckled the bridge, collapsing thousands of pounds of concrete, construction material, cars, and people into the Mississippi River. Her car took an immediate and violent, ten-story dive. Amid a torrent of 111 crashing vehicles, all she could do was grip the wheel and pray.

As soon as her car submerged and the front wheels halted at the bottom, river water surged into her vehicle. Struggling to find an air pocket, she frantically unbuckled her seat belt and pounded on the car windows and roof. Pain and blood seared her hands as the reality of impending death gripped her heart. She thought of her family and hoped they would somehow know she thought of them. Pleading, she called out to God, "Jesus!"

After that, she couldn't remember what happened until she sensed her body floating. Unsure if she was alive or dead, a faint groan filled her throat. Opening her eyes, she noticed a construction worker motioning her toward him. "Over here," he shouted.

"God, help me," she whispered. Could her body swim despite the intense pain in her knees and hands? The man, soaked in mud, ran to a nearby truck and returned with a broom.

Quivering at the sight of her own blood in the muddy water mixed with bridge debris, she forced herself to propel forward, focusing on the rescuer, who stretched himself flat on a steel beam and extended the broom. When she got near enough to grasp the broom, she heard him praying, "Lord, I know You're here. You see us." The man's face was taut, and compassion seemed to rage out of his watering eyes. "Come on," he said to her, "You can do it. Just hold on, and I'll pull you in."

Megan grasped the broom, but a burning sensation in her hands drew an anguished moan, and she let go. After she caught her breath, she tried again and held on. Her face contorted in pain, but she fought through it.

"Good job. We're almost there."

"I'm trying."

"You're doing great."

With one strong, smooth movement and rising to his knees, he pulled her close enough to offer his hand. For the first time since the steel cracked, Megan felt hope. She whispered "thank you" multiple times as he quickly removed her and placed her drenched and shivering body on a rigid bridge remnant. When she saw her blood running down his arm, Megan sobbed.

"You'll be all right now," the man said. "It's a miracle I even saw you. I thought you were dead until you opened your eyes."

"So did I, and I still don't know how I got out of the car."

"Whatever happened, it's obvious you fought hard."

"Yes, I did. I thought of my parents, and I just had to try."

By that time, the paramedics, who noticed the rescue in progress, had run to Megan's side. Gently, they checked her vitals, wrapped her hands, caressed her body in blankets, and transferred her to a firm, black gurney. They asked the man if he was all right. He assured them he was; then, touching Megan's shoulder, he added, "I'll be praying."

On the gurney, Megan beheld the panorama of chaos—firefighters launching rescue boats, parents climbing out of mangled cars clutching their children, people stuck in partially submerged cars, and a school bus overturned on its side with swarms of adults trying to help. Indeed, fatalities lay hidden in the smoke and flames. An initial, eerie quiet had given way to sirens and screams. Then, succumbing to shock, the city of Minneapolis, shrouded in dust, went numb.

As the paramedics shifted her into an ambulance, Megan fixed her eyes on the man covered in mud and blood who was kneeling on steel and bowed in prayer, a visual she never forgot.

By the next day, many of her memories waned and refused to be retrieved. Had it not been for the paramedics, who later visited her and related Megan's trauma to her parents, she would have lost almost all recollection. One of the hardest parts of the ordeal was survivor's guilt. Why did she make it when thirteen did not? Why did she recover so well when others among the 145 survivors suffered extensive injuries?

Never had she been so grateful for faith as in the months that followed, despite multiple surgeries, one on her right knee and both hands. God's grace met her through it all. She had to resign from her dream internship at the Walker Art Center, delay her last year of college by one semester, and wait to start graduate school until January 2009. But, cradling an exciting vision for her Master's in Social Work, she was ready to get started.

No matter what lay ahead, God saved her life with the help of a good man, and no one could take that memory from her.

Two

7:30 p.m., September 22, 2009

Megan loved the way autumn wrapped its benevolent oranges and yellows around maples, oaks, and her all-time favorite, birch trees, a frequent mainstay of her watercolors on cotton canvas. Tonight, though, not even scatterings of bronzed leaves could lift her spirits.

Until a half-hour ago, she had felt positive about her grad school path, but the research grants ceremony derailed her optimism. Surely, she had earned some recognition from Professor Smithton. Instead, he boasted, even lied, "I conceived the idea when the Hennepin bridge collapsed two years ago, and Minneapolis had to recover from a horrible tragedy."

He conceived? That's not the way she remembered it. "I never dreamed he'd claim my idea as his own," Megan whispered. "Use all my hours of research and leave me out of it." She kicked a pile of wayward leaves with gusto. "He told me it would look great on my resume."

Behind her, streaming from the auditorium, the academic elite seemed quiet. When she pulled open the double doors to Einhorn Hall, the hallowed school of social work and her current home away from home, she shook her head and paused at the elevator. "I feel invisible."

Exiting the elevator on the second floor, Megan shivered. The stately, bricked hallway felt cold and empty as she veered left on a familiar trek toward Professor Smithton's office. Since February, she had been alternating research for him with working at Murray's, a local steakhouse where tips added up nicely. But she hadn't been in the office since last Tuesday when the manuscript arrived, and she read the acknowledgments. "Thank you to the fine students who helped along the way with extraneous research."

Extraneous? So much for Minnesota nice, and who were the other "fine" students?

Megan slumped into the huge, well-worn, black leather chair in the assistant's cubby. Surveying the mess of papers, books, and shelves of folders in total disarray, she had no desire to sift through the avalanche of his stuff to organize everything for his convenience.

Then, suddenly, anxiety gripped her chest, a residue effect of the 2007 accident. Her face flushed, and a sensation of fast-falling sucked the breath out of her. "You're all right, Megan," she said. "Breathe. Smithton isn't worth this." Usually, her best recovery tactic with these episodes was to visualize a pleasant memory. Often that memory included her parents, who never failed to give her good counsel. Fortunately, tonight she remembered two of their favorite life philosophies: from her mom, "God the Father sees every good thing you do, even in secret. Don't worry about the applause of people. It's His applause that counts," and from her dad, "Finish what you start. If you can't finish it, don't commit at all."

Megan smiled. The anxiety attack was waning and seemed more like a gift than a struggle. Student chatter shifted Megan's attention back to reality, and she stood up. "Lord, You didn't save me from drowning in the bottom of the Mississippi just to have me waste time and fail," she said. "I believe You see me and know how hard this is. I don't understand, but I will finish my commitment and trust You."

Grabbing a stack of papers, she rolled up her sleeves and cleared the window ledges of Smithton's chess trophies to make room for sorting. As sometimes happened, she noticed the scars on her hands. "Thank you, Lord, for healing me. May these hands serve You well however You want to use them."

Professor Dana Arnold, chair of the Social Work department and professor of Human Behavior and the Social Environment hastened to her Einhorn office as fast as possible, not because she was in a hurry but because she couldn't believe how awkward the awards were, and she needed privacy. When she closed the door, she leaned her back against the wall, shut her eyes, and sighed—a heavy sigh that sounded like a tire going flat from a jagged pile of broken glass shards. Good comparison. She had never worked in a school drenched in so much continuous drama.

Her fiftieth birthday occurred after she and John moved from Indiana in the summer of 2007. Previously, she had served as a graduate director whose primary function was to interact with students. That was a joy, and so was her department head, Pierce Simmons. Thus, when he became Dean of Graduate Studies in a Minneapolis college, she accepted his kind and lucrative offer to join him in administration. Since her son, Peter, was starting law school in the area and John's employment with Apple Computer could transfer to the Mall of America location, everything seemed to line up perfectly.

Much to her dismay, she inherited a nightmare position overseeing a faculty of bitter old-school profs, enthusiastic newcomers, complacent non-vocals, and a few veterans grateful for fresh vision. In particular, a staunch group of malcontents, one of whom had received a plum grant that night, seemed to resist everything she did.

Like a referee in a boxing match, Dana stood between the chaotic social work faculty in one corner and the new dean with his entrepreneurial agenda (as well as connections with deep pockets) in the other corner. Neither side showed much penchant for negotiating.

Dana longed for her student director days when she could work with people of all ages who sought and appreciated her advice. That morning, she had prayed for wisdom yet again, but the day tanked nonstop from the moment she parked until she stood with her back against the wall. Feeling depleted of all energy, she texted John to tell him she was just leaving. "Don't worry about it, hon," he responded. "Peter dropped by, and we're playing cribbage. We're good."

The image of Dad and son playing cards encouraged her. Those two men were her rocks. She couldn't wait to sit down and join them, maybe even play a round of cutthroat. Come to think of it, she might have a better chance of winning in cribbage than the game being played in her department.

Dana grabbed her briefcase and shoved a few files into it

even though she knew the probability of using them overnight was low. Then she remembered the 7 a.m. staff meeting the next morning. Since not-so-friendly fire barraged her all day, she hadn't sent an agenda. Slamming the briefcase on her desk, she sunk into her burgundy leather chair and clicked on the mouse. While waiting for the screen to engage, she read her mouse pad. "Did you ever know that you're my hero? You are the wind beneath my wings."

Dana fingered the pad and cried. Peter gave her that mouse pad for Christmas when he was fifteen. He drew the design of a flying eagle and had one made for each parent. Ordinarily, her mouse pad remained in the backdrop of the mahogany desk and her mind. Wasn't it interesting that it pulled on her attention that night? Peter sang that touching Bette Midler song at the glee club concert. He looked directly at his parents in the audience, prompting John to take Dana's hand; in response, she offered him a Kleenex. *It might have appeared to go unnoticed. But I've got it all here in my heart. I want you to know I know the truth. Of course, I know it. I would be nothing without you.* How she wished she could have had more children, but the one God gave them was so spectacular, she felt as though motherhood had blessed her beyond her dreams.

She smiled and whispered, "Thank you, Lord. I needed that." Within a few minutes, the agenda came together and sped on its way to everyone's email. Pausing again, Dana folded her hands on the mouse pad. "I'm amused, God, because that wasn't exactly subtle," she said. "All my efforts here seem unnoticed. But You know the truth. Of course, You know it."

As Dana locked her office, a group of students bantered in the hallway. "Hey, Professor Arnold, how's it going?"

Although the thought crossed her mind that it was getting

late and they needed to get their lovely selves out of the building, she responded with a smile. "Fine; thanks for asking. Have a good night."

"You have a better one," said a tall red-head she knew from class.

"That's good, Philip. I like that response."

He grinned and tipped his cap a bit. He couldn't have been cuter.

THREE

A soft knock on the door surprised Megan. Unsure whether to answer so late at night, she hesitated, then said, "Who's there?"

"Professor Arnold. May I come in?"

"Of course, Professor!" Megan almost stumbled over the wastebasket already overflowing with trash from a few minutes of work.

When she opened the door, Professor Arnold smiled warmly and looked into her eyes. "Good evening, young lady. What is your name?" Megan hadn't had the pleasure of being in Professor Arnold's classes yet, but she heard their Department Chair was bona fide brilliant and one of the best teachers in the entire school.

"I'm Megan Winfield, and I've been helping Professor Smithton with his research proposal about the Hennepin Avenue bridge collapse." She straightened her blouse and tried to tidy a wayward clump of post-it notes scattered across Smithton's desk.

"Really? I'm sorry. I was not aware of student support for

123

that project." She placed her briefcase by the door. "I have a special interest in that grant." Then, surveying the room, she asked, "Megan, why are you here so late?"

"Well, between my classes and work schedule, this is the only time I've had to give to the project, and I promised Professor Smithton I would clean up the mess we've made in recent weeks."

"Is that right? Hmm." Was that disapproval on the esteemed department chair's face? "And where is he at the moment?"

"I'm not sure, but I believe he said he and the other professors were going to celebrate the grants."

"Of course, that is a worthy cause for celebration, isn't it?"

"Yes, Ma'am."

"Megan, how much time have you put into this project?"

"A lot, about 200 hours."

"Two hundred?"

"Yes, Ma'am."

"Do you have a copy of the proposal, by any chance?"

"Yes, it's right here."

Professor Arnold extended her hand. "May I?"

"Certainly." Megan grabbed the document and wheeled the black leather chair to her.

"That's so kind. Thank you, Megan."

Professor Arnold's tailored clothes mirrored her personality. A red business blazer fit her tall, athletic frame well, covering a navy shift dress trimmed in red that matched leather heels. Rampant student rumors depicted her as a Joan-of-Arc department chair—valiant but besieged by a war she didn't create. Politics, Megan noted, were not uncommon in academia, but she questioned that a woman of this caliber should endure it.

"Is this your only copy?"

"No, we have more."

"I would like to take this with me if you don't mind."

"I don't mind at all. I like that you're interested."

"I'm more than interested, Megan." Grabbing her phone, she said, "Excuse me, please. I need to text my husband."

"No problem."

What was happening? Megan prayed for wisdom. She didn't want to come across as a disgruntled student, although that didn't seem to be a concern. Somehow, she felt peaceful with this woman. Even so, she wasn't prepared for what happened next.

Professor Arnold removed her jacket and her heels, saying, "Please tell me how I can help you, Megan. We're going to get this done so you can go home and get some sleep."

"Oh, my goodness, Professor! You don't have to do that. Really, I'm fine."

"I know I don't have to do it. But I also know I'm looking at a young woman with a ton of character, and I am privileged to be of service to you tonight. Now, please show me what you need, and while we're at it, I'd love to know what you want to do with your life."

Four

When Dana read Smithton's acknowledgments page, she was furious.

She had always felt there was an arrogance about Smithton. Vocal and confrontational, he seemed to be the ringleader of the negative faculty resistance. Despite Megan's composure, Dana smelled student abuse, and she intended to make things right. A sincere, ambitious young woman had poured 200 hours into his project, and he didn't even mention her name.

Unacceptable.

For the next hour, as she worked side by side with Megan, the conversation was delightful. They were a great team, and the place shaped up well. Dana avoided discussing the research project because she wanted to confront Smithton first. To her credit, Megan did not introduce the subject either. This way, since Smithton would probably ask if Megan had complained, Dana could honestly deny it and say she discovered it on her own. Regardless of all those chess trophies, he wasn't the only person in the school who knew how to checkmate an opponent.

At one point, Dana asked Megan about her goals. "What do you want to do with your MSW?"

Megan settled a stack of notebooks on a ledge. She faced Dana. "Professor, my B.A. is in Fine Arts, and my dream is to build a community art center in the urban core to offer art classes and community projects that connect people to each other. I love art and believe in its power to inspire and heal and strengthen human beings. I also think it helps us value what's really important in life, like beauty, hope, and faith in God."

Megan's eloquence impressed Dana. Both the content and delivery reflected a focused heart with a big mission. "Before I comment, would you do me a favor?"

"Of course."

"Please call me 'Dana.'"

"Yes, Ma'am. I will do that as soon as I recover from the surprise." Her eyes widened, followed by a grin of similar breadth.

Dana laughed. "I'm the one who's surprised. This morning in my prayer time (I'm a Christian), I asked God for wisdom for my job. That was the last peaceful moment I had until I walked into this room." Dana sat in Smithton's chair and motioned to Megan. "Why don't you bring your chair over here, so we can talk for a bit?"

"Sounds good." Megan wheeled her chair close to face Dana.

"You love art. I love teaching. I understand your love, and I have a hunch you'll understand mine someday. I trust students. I really do. I trust they want to be better people, learn, grow, and become the special creation God made them to be. If I can be part of that process somehow, I'm thrilled."

Megan nodded, leaning forward, elbows on her knees, chin

in her hands. Her lemongrass blouse tucked into skinny denim jeans that tucked into black, knee-high leather boots. Dana noted the artsy yellow, blue, and orange necklace with hand-painted geometric shapes on cubes. Megan's black hair draped a single French braid down the back.

"I took on administration," Dana said, "not because I'm a substandard teacher, as some surmise about department heads, but because I wanted to support my peers in what they do and also help Dean Simmons with his agenda to prosper the school. But, as I'm sure you've heard, those two goals were at odds before Dr. Simmons and I even arrived."

Resting her arms on her knees, Dana leaned forward toward Megan. "God answered my morning prayer through you. From the moment I began reading that proposal and throughout the past hour, ideas have ruminated in my mind. I see it now. I knew it anyway because of my passion for teaching, but I have fresh clarity. Being here is all about you, the students, and I'm going to finish my tenure with that firm focus at the forefront."

"That's exciting, but Dana," Megan softened her voice. "You've already inspired my life tonight."

"What do you mean?"

"I won't go into it, but I was heartbroken after the awards, and then I remembered my mom—my beautiful, flamboyant mom—who often told me to work for the applause of heaven and my dad who said I should always finish what I start. That's when I went to work, and you knocked on the door."

"Sounds as though you already had a God moment."

"You're right. I did, but there was more He wanted me to realize." Clasping her hands together, she sat up straight. "When you took off your suit jacket and heels, you reminded me of how, at the Last Supper, Jesus dressed as a servant and washed feet. So, Dana, by example, you were Jesus to me tonight."

Dana was speechless, something that hardly ever occurred.

Megan continued, "You're the kind of leader I want to be."

Dana lost all semblance of composure, even trembling a bit. How could she have ever had a better compliment? Or affirmation? It even confirmed Peter's quotation on the mouse pad. She felt humbled.

"Thank you, Megan. You can't begin to know how much that meant to me."

Both women paused. The silence was comfortable. Dana thanked God for His grace and prayed for Megan. Then she noticed the scars on Megan's hands as she had several times during the night.

"Because I care about you, I'm wondering something. If I'm out of line asking this, please forgive me, but would you mind telling me what happened to your hands?"

"No, I don't mind." Megan took a deep breath. "I was on the Hennepin Bridge when it collapsed."

Dana gasped.

"My car plunged into the Mississippi River, and I ripped my hands trying to escape."

"You were literally on the bridge when it went down?"

"I was in the exact middle. I almost drowned."

"I'm so sorry. Wow! I'm so very sorry that happened to you." Dana shivered at the thought. Then she recalled Smithton's comment about conceiving the research premise and wondered if there was more malfeasance on Smithton's part. "Please answer me with a simple yes or no. Is your story in the proposal?"

"Yes."

"Was the bridge collapse part of the primary research question before your involvement?"

"No."

"Thank you. We will leave it at that for now."

"Yes, Ma'am."

"My heart goes out to you. My son was there as well."

"He was?" Megan's eyes widened as she clasped her hands to her face. "Was he all right?"

"Yes, he was working construction that summer before starting law school in the fall. You probably remember four of the eight lanes were closed for various repairs?"

"I do. Thank God for that, right?"

"For sure. I will never forget how I felt when I saw him. All I could do was hug, pray, and cry."

"I understand. Did he have to go to the hospital?"

"No. I suppose you did, though, I mean, for your hands." Observing Megan's hands more closely, Dana surmised there had been some surgery involved as well.

"I did, but it wasn't just my hands. My right ACL was severed, and I went into shock and lost myself for a while." Megan's lips quivered, and Dana's eyes filled with tears. Another silence followed for a few moments. Then, whispering, Megan said, "Your eyes remind me of my hero."

"What hero?"

"A young man rescued me from the water and pulled me to safety. His face is my firmest memory. He was so determined, and he had tears in his eyes the whole time."

"Megan, did he use a broom by any chance?"

"Yes...YES, HE DID. Dana!" Megan jumped up. "Construction worker. . . was YOUR SON my HERO?"

Dana stood up, too, and beamed at Megan. "Yes, I'm proud to say I think he was. I remember now. He said at first he thought you were dead, but then you opened your eyes, and he ran to get something—anything—to extend to you and found a broom. Your courage made him cry because it was excruciating for you to grip the broom. Then he felt as though God wanted him to pray for you, which he did as they carried you to the ambulance."

Megan was sobbing. "May I hug you, please?"

Arms wide open, Dana rushed to her, "Yes, of course! I can't wait to tell Peter."

Megan felt like skipping to her car, as she had so many times when she had made soccer goals as a teen. If Dana hadn't been next to her, she probably would have. What a difference one incredible, godly woman could make in a person's life! Dana insisted on walking with her to the student parking lot to make sure she was safe, and Megan said she would follow Dana to do the same.

Megan tossed her backpack in the backseat and flipped the radio on. "Oh, God. That was so good. Thank you for Dana Arnold in my life, and please, please, please help her with all the junk that's been coming at her. She's your daughter, and such a special one at that." As she backed up, she noticed a few men approaching Dana. She didn't like the looks of it, but she couldn't get up close because Dana had cut through the student parking lanes into the faculty lot. Megan had no other option than to drive down the one-way lane and exit her lot first. Should she get out and run, or would they both be better off with her in a car?

"Oh, my goodness! This is awful. Please protect her. Help us, Lord!"

As she rounded the entrance into the other lot, Dana was getting into the driver's seat. Standing behind her car, obstructing her exit, were Smithton and two other men. At least Megan thought that's who it was, but she couldn't say for sure. When the men saw Megan's headlights, they backed up, and Dana left. Then Smithton and company ambled, rather unsteadily, toward other cars. Megan thought, as long as Dana was safe, she should depart quickly to avoid being identified. Her fast exit precluded another chance to identify the men.

Whatever happened in those couple of minutes was a mystery. At least she could say she saw something happen.

FIVE

6:00 a.m., Thursday, September 23, 2009

Seven a.m. couldn't come soon enough for Dana. Arriving at her office at 6 a.m., she didn't feel the least bit tired. When she came home last night, the first thing she did was call her dean and long-time friend, Pierce Simmons. She shared everything, including the parking lot encounter. They agreed to meet early in the morning because he wanted to read the proposal and attend the staff meeting himself.

As John and Peter listened to Dana's conversation, Dana could see the anger on their faces. Shaking their heads in obvious disbelief, they both paced the room. When she got to the part about the student and her account of the bridge collapse, she didn't include all the details involving Peter because she wanted to stay on task—dealing with a teacher's malfeasance. At that point, the men stopped pacing, and John put his hand on Peter's shoulder. When she finished her conversation, she said, "Okay, that's what happened, but before we talk about that, I have something wonderful to tell you."

"What in the world, Dana?" John looked at her and smiled despite the anger. "I'm not sure what to make of this."

"Just listen. This part is so exciting, and God totally helped me tonight." After she shared the rest of the story, especially the part about the broom, Peter's eyes glistened, "Seriously, Mom? That actually happened?"

"It did, Peter! It had to be you, right?"

"Yes, I don't think I saw anyone else using a broom to pull a woman with bleeding hands out of the river." From his pocket, he removed a chip of concrete from the collapsed bridge that he routinely carried. Rolling it in his hands and grinning from ear to ear, he said, "It amazed me she could even hold on. I've often thought about her. I'm so glad she's all right." He put the chip back in his pocket and clasped his hands behind his head. "And in grad school with a vision like that. I'm impressed."

After that, her two best friends helped her strategize and pray.

Everything was going to change. Smithton may have declared "Check" last night, but the game was on.

As always happened with Pierce, their meeting before the meeting was succinct and productive. When she left her office at 6:30, he was perusing the manuscript. The faculty filed into the Driscoll Conference Room downstairs on the first floor, and Dana opened the meeting on time as usual, even though the Smithton contingent had not yet arrived. She addressed the first four items on the agenda before the latecomers noisily entered. Making no apologies, they interrupted her by continuing their own small talk about what a great night they had celebrating Smithton and his grand achievement.

"Good morning, Professor Smithton," Dana said, "Congratulations are in order."

"Why, thank you very much, Dana." He sat back in his chair and grinned. "How kind of you to notice."

"Oh, I noticed. In fact, I read your proposal."

"I'm honored. Did you like it?"

"Yes," she said. Just then, the door opened again, and Pierce entered the room. Perfect timing.

"Well, good morning, Dean Simmons," Dana said. "What a pleasant surprise!"

Various versions of polite greetings and pleasantries ensued, except from the Smithton contingent, who appeared to squirm in their seats. Pierce pulled up a chair and sat next to Dana at the head of the table. They had planned it that way so that he could say, "I thought I'd drop in this morning and check how things are going around here."

"I was just complementing Professor Smithton on his proposal," Dana said.

"Yes, congratulations, Professor. Nice work."

"Thank you."

"You're welcome. I heard at the ceremony that you conceived the idea of incorporating the bridge when the incident happened."

"Uh, yes. That was an eventful day."

"Indeed, it was. Were you personally involved in the accident?"

"No, I wasn't, but I watched the news."

"As we all did." Pierce motioned to everyone, all of whom complied with a nod.

"I noticed you included one of our own student's account as a source. Her story is riveting. What is her name?"

"You read the whole proposal? Yes, her name is Megan Winfield."

"How did the two of you meet?"

"She was in my Social Policy and Service Delivery class."

"And I gather she must have mentioned the incident in class?"

"No, I invited her to assist with some of the research, and when I mentioned the bridge collapse, she told me."

"How fortuitous."

"Yes."

"So, she did some of the extraneous research you mentioned in your acknowledgments?"

"Yes."

"Did any of the other fine students have an experience similar to hers?"

"Why are you asking?"

"Well, quite honestly, I think it would have been appropriate to acknowledge a student by name whose story you include in the proposal and who assisted with the research. We want to properly reward our students for contributions such as that."

Silence.

"Professor Smithton, do you have a problem with that?"

"Has the student in question complained?"

"Not to me," Pierce answered, looking at Dana.

Everyone jerked their attention to Dana.

"Nor to me," Dana responded, "and no one else brought it to my attention either."

Pierce leaned forward, crossing his arms on the table. "As I said, Professor Smithton, do you have a problem acknowledging a student's service?"

"I think I covered her slight contribution well enough, and, frankly, I don't appreciate the third-degree interrogation."

"Is that right? Well, fasten your seatbelt, Professor. I'm just getting started. Smithton, Harris, and Bradlow, I want to talk to you alone." Then, turning to the other staff at the table, he said, "The rest of you are excused, except for Dr. Arnold. You may stay."

After the room cleared, Pierce continued, "Last night, according to Professor Arnold, the three of you approached her in the faculty parking lot and harassed her, called her gender-abusive vulgarities, and you, Smithton, said, 'Don't mess with me or you'll regret it.' Then, as a group, you stood behind her car to obstruct her ability to leave. Fortunately, another car entered the lane, and you backed off."

"Never happened." Smithton sat back and glared at Dana. "Boy, that's a whopper, Dana." The other two said nothing, shifting their gazes back and forth from Smithton to each other. "We celebrated at Union Station," Smithton continued, "had a few beers and went straight home. She's making that up."

Looking at Harris and Bradlow, Pierce asked, "Is that true? You didn't stop at the school at all?" They nodded, although their stiffness reminded Dana of a certain wooden puppet named Pinocchio. "Professor Arnold," he continued, "all three men deny your story. Do you have a response?"

"Certainly," she said, pulling out her iPhone 3GS, the new release with the first-time-ever video option.

Smithton laughed. "What's with the phone?"

"My husband works for Apple, so we have the latest technology," she said, "just released in June. When I saw you coming, something told me to record you." She turned the phone around and played the video. Checkmate.

Six

Mid-morning, Saturday, October 8, 2011

"I'm beyond excited!" Megan rolled some more orange paint on a 12-inch roller as she applied a second coat to the new community art room at "The Bridge." Two years had passed since that autumn night when she first met Dana, and everything changed in both their lives. All week, she and a special crew had been renovating the charming stucco corner space destined for fulfilling her vision.

Megan loved the new name. Peter thought of it. In fact, he was at her side painting the green trim. "The colors are great, Meg," he said. "I can't wait to do the mural."

"I know . . . I've been dreaming about it." She smiled, not only about the mural but also because she was Peter Arnold's bride.

"You're going to have a lot of fun with those birch trees, aren't you?" He grinned at her.

"Absolutely. What would a "Lakeside Room" be without

birch trees?" She turned to face him, roller dripping a bit. Some orange splats dotted the big denim shirt she bought at the thrift store. "It's really happening, Pete."

"Yes, it is, and God's going to use it."

Megan remembered the prayer she prayed in Smithton's office to use her hands for His glory. "I love everything about this place."

"So do I."

Megan was in a pinch-me-I-must-be-dreaming mode.

In the "Sunshine Room," her grandparents, Pops and Mimi, were painting the walls a gorgeous shade of bright yellow. Meanwhile, the "Snowman Room" was on the agenda for her parents, who were just arriving at the front door. "Hey, sweetie," her mom said, "we've got your preschool tables and chairs in the truck, and you're going to love the invoice."

"Why?" Megan asked, smiling.

"Because it says 'Donated' at the bottom."

"Wow! I wonder if Dean Simmons had something to do with that." Pierce had already landed support and finances from local businesses for them. He and his wife Shirley were family friends and enthusiastic benefactors.

"Want some help?" Peter asked his mother-in-law.

"Yes, that would be wonderful. Thank you."

On the back porch, John was staining a park bench Megan found on eBay, and Dana arranged pumpkins and gourds around the pillars. When she finished, she walked into the Lakeside Room. "This is so beautiful, Megan. Looks like autumn at its best." Dressed in worn jeans and an oversized university sweatshirt, she added, "So, please tell me how I can help you?"

Megan stopped and raised both hands. The roller dripped

more orange, but she didn't care. "That's what you said the night we met."

Dana laughed. "Yes, I didn't realize what I was saying just now until I saw your reaction, so don't give me credit for it."

"Too late. I already did."

A lot had happened since that night in Einhorn Hall. After the tide-turning staff meeting, Dana invited Megan to be her personal assistant, a position that paid so well she didn't need to work two jobs. Working side-by-side with Dana, Megan grew to admire her even more and learned a lot about education, creative administration, and how to be a confident, Christian woman. For that reason, her last day in Dana's office was bitter-sweet in May, but a few weeks later, she had the privilege of becoming Dana's daughter-in-law.

As for the staff problems, Pierce sanctioned the Smithton contingent and put them on probation, after which the rest of the faculty unified under Dana's "Students First" motto. With their support and the dean's endorsement, she implemented a lot of new student-focused policies, among them minimum wage requirements, annual students research awards, and student assistants' awards. From that time forward, all student employment appeared on records, received meticulous over-sight, and required appropriate pay and recognition. She also asked for more funding and source allocations for faculty research, and the grants proposals doubled not only in quantity but in quality. Dana seemed to have come into a new season in her life, where all her skills and gifts merged in remarkable cohesion.

As a result, Megan followed Dana's example and named her mission "Community First." August 1, 2007 had left marks on Megan's hands and soul, but through the smoke and chaos of grief, God the Father called her and rewarded her faith with a life purpose that suited her in every way. Flashbacks were almost nonexistent, and her respect for an all-seeing God had grown to a new level of trust and intimacy. Under His direction and providence, tragedy had transformed into destiny.

That night at The Bridge, as the family gathered in the Lakeside Room to eat and admire their handiwork, including the mural still in process, Dana started giggling, "Peter, that's brilliant. I love the way you hid that."

"I figured you'd pick up on it first, Mom."

Wondering what she missed, Megan walked up to the mural to study Peter's part, primarily the bridge. Then she saw it. "Perfect," she said, beaming at her husband. "Beautifully done."

There, in the middle of the bridge, he had hidden three words on the surface. Appearing as a mixture of golden light beams and gray shadows on dark wood planks, the calligraphy burst through an autumn sunrise and said, "The Father Sees."

After the others deciphered the message, Megan's hero, who had rescued her from the Mississippi River with a broom and a prayer, held her in his arms in front of the mural. John took a picture with his phone, and a grateful family offered thanks to God.

Although Megan had never figured out how God got her out of a flooded car, she knew He saved her and would never abandon, forget, or ignore her. She was visible to Him, and His faithfulness and applause were all that would ever matter.

Deva's Divine Design

by Janet Oliver

JANET L. OLIVER'S writing career started early with her groundbreaking work in the field of neurodevelopment. Later her research and writing became interwoven with her love of Christ. Janet's writing often explores the relationship of God's developmental design and His plan for each of us. As a mother of four grown daughters, she has personal and professional experience with the challenges of life in this postmodern age.

In addition to this theme, she also writes historical Christian fiction about the lives of the extraordinary Christian followers through the ages. Janet lives in Chanhassen, west of the Twin Cities, with her husband, tending her garden and working with people of all ages with sensory-motor issues through developmental approaches.

jloliverchauthor.blogspot.com/
www.planforlearning.com

 facebook.com/Storiesforadventurouschristians

One

New Year's Eve was a blast! He swam straight over to her, so happy to have finally found her! Definitely a match made in heaven. Yeah, he was vaguely aware of others, but he seemed to know, as she knew, that God had put them together.

When they joined, a whole new season began! Together, they made me complete. God brought into being a unique design of hundreds of characteristics. Me!

Laura awoke and looked over at Rory's tousled black hair and shivered in the cold Minnesota morning. She had definitely had too much to drink last night, but she remembered his gentle, warm touch. She ached so much for that. To finally be seen, she had to take a little risk. She had felt attractive for the first time in her life! She felt, could she even say it? She felt loved.

Laura quickly bound her messy blond hair into a ponytail

and looked out into the frozen landscape that was beginning to whiten in the dawning light. Who was she kidding? She got nailed at a one-night stand. No one can fall in love at a New Year's Eve party. She totally fell for that emergency medical technician line of his. Laura felt the shame well up, tightening her chest and pushing hot tears down her cheeks. Silently, she slipped on her boots and pulled her coat over her underwear. She grasped pieces of her clothing she found on the floor and gripped her coat tightly around her bare body. Ready to face the blast of Minnesota's arctic air, she silently slunk out his door. Rory's door.

I settled into the wet, warm, dark, and muffled place. Ah, I could feel the multiplication of the cells after I attached them to the wall. Slowly, I got organized. Within a dozen short weeks, I could touch myself and other stuff around me. I could taste the salty liquid. At times, a glow of light would appear out of the soft darkness. But best of all, as small as I was, I could stretch and flip in the buoyant lightness of my being.

But what is that?

I hear muffled sounds. Sad sounds. I don't know how I know these sounds are sad. But these are hauntingly sad sounds. Up to now, I have been so happy. Now I sense sadness.

Laura sobbed until her body throbbed, thinking, *Just my luck! Just my stinkin' luck.* She had to face it. She hadn't had her period in some time. She looked out at the heaving glacier of ice in the yard in front of her place. It creaked and cracked like a broken heart.

The March rawness of Minnesota radiated from the panes of window glass in her room. She hadn't been with anyone since that beautiful night with Rory. The memory of that encounter brought all the sensations back to her. How he laced his fingers in hers and gently wiped her hair from her face to kiss her. His warm and loving embrace. She had felt so safe. Now, where was he? Where was she? Alone. As always.

When Laura was six, her heroin-addicted father had realized that heroin was his hero, and he needed no other mistress. He left without a glance backward. Laura's mother tried to keep it together for another few years, but she succumbed to the street life as well. After that, it was a string of foster homes until her emancipation. Laura was determined that she would break this family curse. No drugs. Be careful. Be in control. Don't slip. Trust no one.

But here she was. She added up the details one by one. Feeling fat plus sore breasts equals....pregnant. She had thought the nausea was the flu. What could she do? The best thing to do was face the truth and call Planned Parenthood. Laura reached for her phone. Through her tears, she found the website and pressed the numbers.

Two

"Planned Parenthood," she heard the overly chipper female voice reply. To her surprise, her voice sounded steely and cold as she made the appointment for her abortion. "It won't cost you a thing," the chirpy voice said.

Sure, it wouldn't cost her a thing.

She was awake all that night and the next day. Laura called in sick to her low-paying job at the coffee shop. Between her nausea and self-loathing, she watched the weak March Minnesota sunshine muster up enough energy to melt the icicles hanging dangerously off the roof of her rooming house. She bundled up and went out into the yard that was filled with dirty snow and heard the sound of sirens split the air. Laura shivered, and again tears filled her eyes.

She thought of her second, or was it her third foster home? That was the one with Mama Genene and Papa Tyree. It was a brief, but rare, happy moment in Laura's life, until Papa Tyree's heart attack. They were the genuine article. Kind but firm.

They read the Bible to her every day. They talked about how God loved her. But they, too, had left her.

She looked up into the sky. *God, if you are out there, I need help! I am alone. Where are you? Why do you hate me so much?* Laura scrubbed her eyes with her cold hands as she slowly walked toward the gate to the street.

Laura hated this early spring in Minnesota, and now it would forever be cursed by her memory of the abortion-to-be. Her mind thought of Rory. The baby (should she use that word?) was his too. He'd never even know. She had not tried to contact him after that night.

She shivered again, and once more, she beseeched God, "If you are there, give me a sign." Laura opened the gate to the sidewalk. As she moved through the gate, something by the side of the hedge caught her eye. *What is that?* Laura thought. She backed away from the beckoning gate and moved toward the tiny green and white apparition. She leaned over but felt a rush of nausea. Giving in to gravity, Laura knelt on the cold, slightly melting spot.

She could not believe her eyes! There were not one but three white bells hanging off tiny green stalks. All around them, tiny green spikes of the flowers' leaves poked bravely through the crystalline snow. So these must be the flowers that people call snowdrops. How could something so fragile and beautiful exist in the harsh Minnesota March? But they were defying the odds.

Just then, she heard the bells from St. Bart's Church. Suddenly, she realized that it must be Lent. Easter was coming soon! Jesus's resurrection. The knees of her jeans were wet and cold. But she had her answer. She reached for her phone. The same overly cheerful voice sang out, "Planned Parenthood. How can we help you?"

I love my fingers! I can grab my cord! I can suck my thumb! I am so happy again.

The sound of sad crying is less often now.

I can do somersaults. Whee! Uh oh! All those gyrations gave me hiccups! Oh, bother! They shake me all over.

Laura laid back and suddenly started. The nurse helped her put her legs in the stirrups. "What's wrong, dear?" Laura looked in amazement at her broadening midsection. It was jerking at rhythmic intervals. The nurse laughed. "That little one has hiccups! That is totally normal. The doctor will be in soon." With that, she walked out.

Laura lay in this obscenely ridiculous position and looked out the window into the greening trees. The leafing trees of May made Laura glad. Things were looking up.

The doctor entered, and after chastising her for not coming in for a prenatal checkup earlier, he told her that she was about six months on. After doing an ultrasound and thumping her here and there, he pronounced her and the baby to be in better condition than her behavior might warrant.

Things were better than she had imagined that dreary winter day three months ago. The coffee shop had allowed her to keep her job, even though she had told them that she was pregnant, which was very embarrassing. Everyone was nice and all, but most knew she was not married and didn't even have a boyfriend.

They temporarily changed her hours to the evening shift so she could go to her GED classes at St. Bart's Church. After hearing their bells ring repeatedly, she had finally called them for help. They had a program to help young women with unplanned pregnancies finish their high school education. What a change in her heart and hope!

The nurse at St. Bart's free clinic didn't pull any punches. She told her the options, and she was obviously of the opinion that Laura should allow the baby to be adopted by a two-parent family. Laura had known she would be faced with this choice. But just as she couldn't face being pregnant, and she couldn't quite face a doctor, now she couldn't choose between keeping or giving her baby up for adoption. Again, her tears surged.

THREE

The nurse clucked, "There, there, you don't have to decide right now. Think about it. Talk to your family and friends, and even your pastor. I just want you to be thoughtful of the time and money a child takes for a single parent."

Laura left and walked outside, feeling the warming sun and the cool air against her cheeks. She had no one to talk to about this. No one. Her parents were gone with the wind. She had moved last Christmas from San Francisco to Minneapolis to escape the looming possibility of homelessness. Then she remembered the sign of the snow bells. She sighed and sat on a park bench, facing the sun.

"Lord, I now know you are there, and you have a plan. I don't know what that is! Do I keep the baby and risk a life of poverty? Or do I do the noble thing and give another couple the chance to love my baby?" Laura realized that her hands were clasped in prayer on her baby bump. She just heard the wind rustling the newly formed leaves in the trees. "I have time to think about this. Lord, bless this child I am carrying."

What had up until recently seemed like endless space is now tight and restricting. I try to stretch and turn, but I am repelled by a tight, elastic boundary.

What is going on here? I need my space!

I open my mouth and drink in the fluid. I used to love this place, but now I am beginning to think there is more to my existence than these limits.

But what is next?

When the time comes, will I know what to do?

Laura looked at her calendar as she heaved herself out of her small bed. Where was the time going? Fall was in the air. She had to decide about the baby. At work, everyone just expected her to keep the baby. Why not? It wasn't the end of *their* lives.

She stood and urgently needed to pee. She barely made it to the toilet with the baby bearing down on her bladder. She was tired again. She felt the time had to be near. She wanted her body back. She wanted her freedom.

Laura looked around her hole-in-the-wall room. What was she thinking? She had hardly made any of the preparations she needed for living with a newborn. There was no extra cash for even the basic needs of a baby. She wasn't ready for an infant in her life. That must be the sign. Her lack of readiness showed her that she could never be a mother alone. She didn't know what she was doing. This baby deserved a better life. She would sign the adoption papers at her next visit to the clinic. She glanced at the clock and realized that she had to move it or be late for her next shift at the shop.

She thought and prayed as she walked to the coffee shop. The first few yellow leaves of autumn swept past her feet. Minnesota's warm seasons were so short. But the coolness of fall would be a comfort in this end stage of pregnancy. The bell tinkled as she walked into the shop. Workers and customers alike gave her a warm wave. They seemed happy to see her.

She put on her apron and found the straps no longer reached around her enough to tie. One of her colleagues came up behind and used a chip clip to hold the apron. Laura wanted to smile and thank her, but she was still feeling a bit walled off from the world. She began to wipe the counter as she waited to fill the next order.

"What would you like?" asked the order-taking barista.

"I'd like a dark roast medium with room for cream," said a deep voice. "Laura? Is that you?"

Laura turned to see the tousled black hair of Rory. Laura wanted only to melt away into the floor. She uselessly threw her arms over her bump, almost tipping the latte she was holding.

"Oh my God, Laura!" cried Rory.

Laura hung her head and headed for the back-alley door. Outside, dark clouds brewed in the west. She covered her face with her hands as she leaned her side against the brick exterior of the shop.

In a few moments, she felt warm, firm hands grasp her shoulders. She wanted to both contract into a black hole, and, at the same time, to melt into those beautiful hands. The hands turned her and she looked into the chocolate brown of Rory's eyes.

"Laura, what happened? You just disappeared! I didn't even have your phone number before you left," Rory said with pain in his voice.

Laura's pent-up anger and self-hatred welled up and burst into the alley. "Well, you have eyes, don't you?" Laura felt all the shame, hurt, and fear flow out of her. "Not that you have to care."

Rory pulled her over to the two wire alley chairs that acted as the shop's smoking lounge. "Laura, I do see. Am I the father?"

As she sat, she faced away from Rory. "What do you think?"

"Well, I don't know. That's why I asked. Obviously, you have had time to adjust to this. I had no idea," he said defensively.

There was a pause, and the wind blew a couple of wet drops onto their heads. Laura leaned with her elbows on the rickety arms of the wire chair. She again dropped her head. Her heart burned within her. Suddenly, a large gray squirrel jumped on the cigarette sand bucket and started to dig in the wet sand fanatically.

Rory laughed, and the tension broke. "What is he doing?" he asked.

Laura stared at the fury and determination of the squirrel. "He is preparing for the winter by burying nuts," replied Laura.

"Where did he come from, do you think?" Rory glanced up the alley.

"He had to have come a long way. He took a risk to find just the right place for his stash," Laura mused. She was calmer now. "Look, Rory, I didn't think I'd see you again. I'm sorry if I have put you on the spot."

Rory's eyes moved from the digging squirrel to Laura. "Laura, I have been looking for you for months and months. All I had for a clue was a coffee shop receipt that must have dropped from your pocket that night. Do you know how many Moose Bucks Coffee shops there are in this city?"

"You were looking for me?"

"Yes, of course. I know our meeting at that New Year's Eve party was random. But I want you to know, I don't take every girl I meet home with me! I thought I must have offended you or something," Rory said sadly.

"No, Rory, I really felt close to you, but I couldn't believe the feelings could be two-way. I don't sleep around, and that I let myself slip, slip and be caught...." Laura looked down at her prominent bump.

"Laura, you should have come to me. This must have been hell for you! I'm surprised that you didn't go for an abortion. To free yourself from the pain, I mean." Rory stammered.

Laura crossed her arms against the chilling wind. "I almost did. I know it sounds silly, but I think God sent me a sign."

Rory took off his EMT jacket and slipped it around her.

"A sign? From God?" Rory sat next to her again.

"You'll think me silly, and maybe I was just looking for an excuse, but in March, I was going to have an abortion. I discovered these beautiful, precious snowbell flowers in my yard, and then I heard the Lenten church bells, and well...it seemed providential."

Rory looked surprised. "That is an amazing story. I am not a materialist. I believe that God or the power of existence or whatever speaks all around us. I think you were right."

Laura smiled, and Rory saw the delicate beauty that she always seemed to want to hide. "I need to get back to work. The others have to make up for any breaks."

"No problem, but this time I want at least your phone number. You are not getting away from me that easily again," he said with a grin.

Laura stood basking in his grin and said, "I guess you need this really cool jacket back. You really are an EMT. Of course..."

Just then, she felt something warm flowing down the inside of her legs. *Am I peeing myself?* thought Laura. But then she felt it, a sudden, strong pull around her middle. *Oh no,* she thought. *Is this it? This is it!* The shock overcame her fear.

Four

What was that? Uh oh, something strange is happening.
I feel a pull. Something is pulling me downward!
Where am I heading?
What comes after this?

~

Rory looked at her with concern. "Laura, are you OK?"

"The baby is coming!" she said, almost shouting, and her head began to swirl. "Owww," she cried as she slumped back into the chair.

That squeezing is not fun! What does this mean?

Now Rory jumped up. "I'll get help! You stay here!"

Laura wanted to tell him to stay, but the next pain started. She grimaced in agony.

~

I didn't know the season when I slithered down the seemingly eternal passage. But I felt an alien force hit my limbs. It felt like a heavy, thick blanket was lying on me. I did my best to rail against the pressure of the air, the coldness, and the brilliant light that was so different from my recent and only experience inside.

Soon I felt a snug embrace, and a warm softness entered my mouth, and equally warm liquid filled me up in my center.

Then my body succumbed to the heavy air and fell into a deep sleep.

Laura tiredly pulled herself up and saw Rory holding up the swaddled baby. At first, she wanted to shout at him to be careful, but then she saw the rapture and awe in his face. "Laura, look, she has my eyes! And she has your lips!"

"She does?" Laura laughed, even in her exhaustion and pain. Rory looked like a kid at Christmas. He brought the bundle over and leaned over to show her the baby's big chocolate-brown eyes and her bow-shaped mouth. *My mouth cannot be this beautiful,* thought Laura.

The nurse stepped in. "Everything going alright with Mom, Dad, and babe? That was a speedy birth, but you all did great. I need to take that little one in for a few standard requirements. Sorry, Dad, you will have to stop loving on that baby for a few minutes." Laura flushed with chagrin over the nurse's assumption of everyone's relationship.

Rory gave the baby over with seeming reluctance. The nurse took the little bundle and said, "I'll be back soon to ask you her name. I'm sure you've thought of a great one."

Laura looked horrified. She hadn't picked a name! What kind of mother was she? A name, a name. What kind of name should she choose?

Rory broke abruptly into her thoughts. "Let's name her Deva! It's my grandmother's name. She's southern, and she tells everyone that it means 'divine.' It just seems right."

Laura felt her thoughts fall out of the bubble around her head. Rory had just named her baby. She meant *their* baby. He wanted to name the baby after his grandmother. What could this mean? Was he taking her baby? No, of course not. He was assuming that he would be a part of Deva's life.

Did I just name the baby Deva? Laura asked herself.

Rory went on, "I know it's an unusual name, and maybe you want something else, but she sure looks like a Deva." He turned eager, questioning eyes toward Laura.

"I don't know what to think! You didn't even know I was pregnant until today, and you want to name the baby? Don't get me wrong. I think that's great, but this all seems to be moving very fast. You can just walk out if you want."

Rory pursed his lips as if thinking. "Fast dating, fast birth, fast naming, yes, it has been a bit of a whirl, but I'm actually enjoying what life is laying down. What if I don't walk out?"

"Being a parent doesn't freak you out?"

"Yes, but no. Life's curveballs aren't so bad if you have some faith. I'm game if you are. We can go as slowly as you want, but here we are. I think one either accepts where things are in life, or one avoids things. I find avoiding usually doesn't help," said Rory.

Laura thought of all the ways she had been avoiding life. Maybe Rory was right. Perhaps, with some faith, she could stop avoiding situations and embrace them. That would definitely be easier with help. Help. That was a foreign word for Laura. Then she heard a voice from beyond say, "Helpmeet."

Laura repeated the word out loud, "Helpmeet."

"That's an old word. I think it's from the Bible. Something about it not being good for people to be alone. We all need help, Laura. Let's meet to help this kid have a good life," suggested Rory.

The nurse came in pushing a cart with a baby bed on top. "What a little angel. No fussing at all." She took out the clipboard at the end of the cart. "So, do you have a name yet?"

Laura looked at Rory and said, "Yes, Deva."

The nurse nodded. "That's a lovely name. Deva. D E V A?"

FIVE

After many cycles of thrashing, feeding, and sleeping, I began to make sense of my place and position in this strange world. I was a soul in an absurdly small and often disagreeable body. Thankfully, I also had others around me. The central figure was the source of my nutrition and rest.

When the discomfort of my world, whether cold, wetness, lights, hunger, or sounds, became too much, this being was there for me. I recognized her first from her scent. She smelled of my delicious milk, but she also gave that life-filled love that bathed me.

Just before Christmas, I knew that she was my mother. She and the big person with his strong smell, who was my father, helped me to explore my small world.

~

"Look at all those beautiful lights, Deva," cooed Rory. He held her up to see the Christmas tree. "They twinkle, but not like you do!"

"Oh, Rory! You are going to make her think she is the queen of the universe if you keep that up!" Laura said as she sat on the new couch, a gift from Rory's grandmother. When she called after it arrived, Grandmother Deva had said, "That namesake of mine needs a place to sit!"

Laura was exhausted with night-time feeding and dealing with a fussy baby. She was conflicted with both happiness at Rory and his family's embrace and the constant gnawing feeling that it was all too good, and it would all soon be taken away. After all, she hardly knew Rory. She didn't even know herself.

Rory looked over and said, "We need to get ready to go to St. Bart's for our pre-marital counseling."

"Rory, I am so exhausted! Do I have to go?" pleaded Laura.

"I'll get Deva ready and in her seat. All you need to do is be in the car in fifteen minutes," Rory said.

"Rory! I look terrible. I need to shower and do my hair!" argued Laura.

"Laura, you have never looked better! The pastor won't care. We promised we would come after all they've done to help," said Rory, trying to hold back a bit of exasperation.

Laura looked at Rory again, cooing at Deva as he walked to the changing area set up in the alcove. Again, the conflicting feelings welled up of love for his leadership and care and her own gripping need to control the situation. "Lord, help me!" she said, and then with an effort, she stood and walked to the bathroom.

In the pastor's small office, they sat talking about their lives.

Laura's shame covered her as she tersely told of a life of neglect and abandonment. Both the pastor and Rory listened intently.

After she had finished, the pastor thanked them for their honesty. Then, he prayed for each in turn. Before they left, the pastor handed each of them a pamphlet from a side table. "You are both moving very quickly into a new world of marriage and parenting. Unfortunately, both of you have also had traumas around your parents. This affects how young couples deal with each other and a baby. I strongly suggest that you both talk to a counselor about the effects of these personal issues. Here is a Christian psychologist that works with us often."

Laura was about to hand the pamphlet back to the pastor with a retort that she wasn't mentally ill and how could he assume such a thing when Rory said, "I think this is a great idea! My insurance will pay for me, so we'll just figure out Laura's."

"If you need any financial help, we have a fund. I am really delighted at your mature reaction. I see the Lord working in every part of your lives," said the pastor as he walked to the office door. "We'll all be praying for you here at St. Bart's."

Outside as Rory put Deva in her car seat, Laura wanted to cry and yell. In a smoldering voice, she said, "What makes you think I need mental help?"

As Rory got into the driver's seat, he gave a surprised look at Laura. "If your heart stopped, wouldn't you want a cardiologist? If your heart has been broken, you need a psychologist. At least that's what I think."

Laura paused. Did she have a broken heart? Yes. Over and over again. Could she lay all that out to a stranger? Rory continued, "I actually need to talk about me. I'm a dad now. You heard me tell the pastor about how my dad left my mom when I was a baby. The man I call Dad is my stepfather. I know that shouldn't matter, but it does; I can feel it. Do you feel all the hurt from your childhood?"

Laura bowed her head and tried not to cry. "Yes, but I can handle it myself."

"One thing Grandma Deva used to say, '*Trust in the LORD with all your heart and lean not on your own understanding.*' I used to make fun of Grandma for all of her Bible talk, but I keep seeing God's hand in my life and in yours. Funny, how babies change a person's point of view." Rory said as they drove toward home.

After Rory parked the car, Laura put her hand on Rory's. "I'm sorry for my reaction. I want to feel God in my life more. I need to learn how to lean on God more. I am just not used to it. Be patient with me."

Rory turned to her and kissed her softly. "Only if you overlook my own cluelessness."

And then, in almost a whisper, she said, "I love you."

"That's a relief since we're getting married on New Year's Eve! One year ago we met; I fell in love at first sight. Can we do this together and love Deva?"

"Only if we don't lean on our own understanding, I guess," said Laura sheepishly.

New Year's Eve was a blast! Definitely, this is a match made in heaven. I knew that God had put us all together.

When they married, a whole new season began! Together he and she with God made me complete.

Me, Deva!

Winter Sky Crasher

by Donald Roome

DONALD ROOME retired as an RN in 2012 and then worked with his wife as a missionary to Muslims until 2020. He has children and grandchildren scattered throughout the USA. He began writing fiction in 2003, and because he wrote about a Muslim terrorist, he used Jacob S. Wells as a pseudonym to avoid problems while traveling in Muslim countries. His first novel, Death of a Terrorist is the story of a young man who becomes a terrorist because of America's corrupting influence on his sister, but he eventually finds salvation through Christ and puts his anger to death on the cross.

Don currently focuses on evangelism through his local church, prayer ministries, and writing fiction and nonfiction. He is currently is blogging about his experiences walking the Camino de Santiago. You can read more about Don, his novel and his other writings at HowGodisheard.com.

facebook.com/donald.roome.3

ONE

"Ole, wake up! Breakfast is ready," Mamma's soft voice beckoned me.

The sun was shining through the frost-caked window. With a bedroom window that faced south in Minnesota in December, that can only mean that it had to be well past the time morning chores should have been done. The whinny of horses and Father's soothing voice came from the barn. *For sure, Father isn't letting me sleep late because he is forgetting to take me to the ski jump. Maybe some urgent business requires him to go later and stay longer, so he has to leave me behind. I should be so lucky.* The heat from the stove in the central room in the house had already taken most of the chill out of the bedroom. My brother, Lars, who was eight years younger than me, was already out of bed and out of sight. My sister, Olga, was jabbering with Mamma in the kitchen.

I put on my coat and boots and rushed through the kitchen, so I could get outside to the outhouse to relieve myself.

"Good morning, sleepyhead," Olga called. "Are you going to greet us or maybe thank us for letting you sleep late?"

"Thanks for letting me sleep late," I yelled outside the entrance to our home. The snow was almost half a foot deep and the temperature was a little below freezing, perfect weather for skiing. While inside the outhouse, I could hear scraping sounds coming from the barn, from what must have been Lars' shovel as he mucked the cow and sheep stables. *It sounds like Lars is doing my morning chores.* I shrugged. That wouldn't help me escape the ski jump.

When I returned inside, Olga handed me a wash basin with water partially warmed from the stove. I grinned at her. "Wow! You are treating me like royalty."

"Pappa is eager to get to town, so he can have ample time to watch the ski riders," Olga chatted as she stuck more wood in the stove. "I wish I could go with you and watch the skiers fly through the air with the grace of an eagle, but Pappa said that you were the only one he wanted to go with him."

Taking a deep breath, I stood still considering the full implications of what that meant. When he was fifteen, a year younger than I was, he was taught by the Hammestvedt brothers for whom the label of *sky crashers* was first coined. The familiar smell of smoldering pine and the kitchen's warmth failed to ground my mind in today. Father had high hopes for me, and having little I could do about it, I walked to my bedroom in silence and set the basin on the commode. *Sure, Father only wants me with him, so he can coax me into loving the sport of ski jumping.* My heart's desire was to do anything but ski off a ramp and fly in the air, leaving my stomach some-where behind. Instead of crashing through the sky, all I could think of was crashing on the ground with my legs and arms sprawled in opposite directions. After washing, I returned to the kitchen, and Mamma put a partial loaf of dry bread and a dish of milk at my usual place at the dinner table. She left me a nice-sized portion of the loaf. Before reciting the prayer we say before eating, I silently asked God for the grace to survive the ski jumps later today. After thanking the Lord for his provision, I tore a piece off of the loaf, and being in a contemplative mood, I slowly dabbed the piece in the milk, making sure it was thoroughly soaked.

Mamma scowled at me as she stood at the kitchen counter kneading the dough for some bread. "Ole, don't dawdle. You know how anxious your father is to get to town."

I nodded and promptly stuffed the sopping piece in my mouth and swallowed. "Then why did he let me sleep late?"

Mamma shrugged and put the dough in a large bowl. "Why don't you ask him? I imagine he wanted you to be as thrilled about the beginning of the ski season as he was, and he hoped that sleeping late would perk you up... and... perhaps, help you enjoy seeing Red Wing's return to the glory days when we were called the *sky crashers*."

That was undoubtedly true. I tore off another piece of bread in silence and soaked it lazily. *Doesn't Father realize that the thought of ski jumping terrifies me?* Making Father wait because I dawdled, however, didn't make me feel any better. After breakfast, I found Father standing behind the gate next to our two gray Percheron draft horses, adjusting the harnesses that connected them to the buckboard. He turned to me when I was about ten feet away and smiled. "Did you enjoy the extra sleep?"

I nodded. "Yeah, thanks." *Don't expect that to change my attitude about skiing off a ramp.* I climbed up onto the buckboard seat and glanced back at the wagon bed loaded with rough lumber and a blanket covering some bags and what looked like bags and skis. "What's in the bags?"

Father handed me the reins and hopped up next to me. When he had finished settling in, he grabbed the reins back from me. "Underneath are bags of corn for the general store to trade for some supplies, and your mother has some quilts that she made for Mrs. Schmidt." He flicked the reins, and the horses trotted at a pace that reflected the excitement in Father's mood.

I hung on as we bumped over the frozen ruts in the road. *Well, if we get to Red Wing quicker, my time worrying will be shortened and the torture less protracted, but this isn't helping my stomach settle much.* Breakfast felt like it was curdling a little more with each bump, but the crisp air in my face spurred me on and helped keep nausea somewhat at bay.

Two

Plumes of frosty breaths puffed from the horses' nostrils as they trotted briskly until we reached the main road a mile from town, and then Father slowed them, relaxing on the more traveled road. In town Father occasionally stopped the horses as we met others who were out running errands. Normally, he would have chatted at length with whomever was willing to discuss the weather, how the crops were growing, or how their family was doing.

Today he cut short his conversations. Our first stop in town was at the lumberyard to trade our debarked tree trunks for a few white pine and white oak planks. Our next stop was Carl Elk's shop where Mr. Elk made and sold skis.

Mr. Elk was in a talkative mood. "Sure, I can use some white oak and white pine planks." Father and Mr. Elk each grabbed a few planks and went into the shop, haggling over the value of the planks.

After waiting a few minutes sitting on the buckboard seat, I became bored, so I hopped off and walked down the street towards the high school. A classmate from school saw me and chatted at length about joining the ski club. Skiing was not a subject I wanted to discuss. As soon as I could politely free myself from our conversation, I did.

Father and Mr. Elk were already standing by our buckboard, so I ran to join them and hopped onto the buckboard seat.

Mr. Elk leaned against our buckboard and slapped me on my thigh as we sat on the seat. "Ole, come by the Bush Street Hill in a couple of hours. I'll be giving some of the younger guys tips on jumping with good form."

I nodded and tried to smile.

Father flicked the reins and we headed to the general store. Talking with Mr. Elk seemed to animate Father's voice. "Ole, the youth in Red Wing have an opportunity to learn skiing from one of the best skiers in the nation. Ho, the Aurora Ski Club will be back in full force to what it was ten years ago. Look, the whole town is getting excited about watching the revived sky crashers."

I scoffed. "Do you really think the town is that excited about it?" *Would the whole town be there to watch me?*

"Why wouldn't they? We have some of the best skiers in the country right here." Father nodded with his whole upper torso.

"Sure, of course." *You believe that I am going to be one of the best in the nation, too.* My stomach churned, making me wish the horses would slow down even farther.

"You sound doubtful, son. We already have plenty of snow, the temperature is perfect, our boys have skis made from shops right here, and a history of producing champions. Why shouldn't our town get excited about this season?"

"I suppose." *You think that if I am trained in Red Wing, a town with a history of winners, that I will be a champion skier, as well.*

Father nudged me with his shoulder. "Even if no one else is excited, you and I can certainly enjoy taking in the season together."

"Ya, sure, you betcha," I replied, trying to sound a little enthusiastic. *You watching and me crashing doesn't sound enjoyable.... It sounds more terrifying and stomach wrenching.*

In a few minutes, we arrived at the general store. Father threw supplies into the wagon bed while I browsed through the store, hoping to distract my mind from the impending disaster on my skis. On the way out to join Father, I bumped into Leif, a neighbor and school chum. "How are you doing?" I stammered, surprised to see him in town.

"I am meeting Carl Elk at Buck Street Hill as soon as I am done running errands." Leif kept talking as he headed toward the hardware section. My father will be helping my aunt until evening. Come join the rest of us at Bush Street!"

"I'll be there," I called back. *Though I sure wish I wasn't.*

THREE

Father was sitting on the buckboard seat when I got outside. A few minutes later, we were at Mrs. Schmidt's and delivered Mamma's quilts. After we had unhooked the horses, fed and cared for them in her stable, we joined her in her parlor to socialize while we waited for her to serve us a supper of sauerkraut and sausage which she had promised to give us as partial payment for the quilts.

Mrs. Schmidt was a kind, lonely widow, and I tried to engage in polite conversation. Though I was relieved at first when she announced that the meal was ready and that we should come to the dining room, I soon thought otherwise. The food tasted funny and made me feel nauseated, though the problem was probably with my gut and not the food.

After we had chatted another hour, I started to feel like I might lose my food, so I excused myself to use her toilet.

Her indoor plumbing was beautiful with brass fixtures that were framed by intricately embroidered pink towels and curtains. The thought of soiling anything or making any offensive smells or noises gave me incentive to squelch any sensations of vomiting.

I took a deep breath and gazed out her window. The snow looked like it was melting. Maybe the snow would become unsuitable for skiing. That would be a miracle.

When I returned to Mrs. Schmidt's dining room, Father announced that we had to leave.

After we thanked her and excused ourselves, we hooked up our horses and headed to the Bush Street Hill. Father seemed to be in a contemplative mood, and we rode in silence until we arrived at the Post Office, our last stop before Bush Street Hill. Father ran into the Post Office while I waited with the horses. When he returned it became apparent that he must have talked with someone in the Post Office, for he hopped up onto the buckboard seat and laughed.

"You should hear what people are saying. The Red Wing boys are going to bring back the glory days of the *sky crashers*. Ha, I was once one of their young, bright shining stars, learning to fly like the Hemmestvedts themselves."

"Yeah, I was five years old, but I remember." *And now you expect me to be a shining star that learns to fly like Carl Elk. I* nodded as Father flicked the reins, and the horses trotted away at a brisk pace.

What I had been dreading ever since the leaves had turned brilliant fall colors was upon me. Shortly, we turned onto Bush Street, and Father pulled gently on the reins, slowing slightly the horses to a safer pace as we neared people walking, most of whom were headed toward the hill as well.

One block before the hill, we passed Leif. "Hey, Ole, wait for me! Don't go down the hill until I get there."

Father kept going, and I looked at Leif and shrugged. *I*

would have been glad to wait for you. In fact, I would be glad to wait all afternoon at the bottom of the hill and watch every jump you make while I sit and watch you.

Father glanced at me and smiled. "Leif will catch up quickly and have all afternoon to ski. Oh, Ole, this is such a beautiful time of year. Are you as excited as I am?"

I swallowed hard. "Yeah, sure." *For you it might be beautiful, but you expect me to fly like a Hammestvedt off the ramp.*

A half a block away the steep hill was plainly visible. The afternoon sun glistened on the icy snow covering the runway, showcasing its potential for speed and terror. A skier raced down the hill, off the ramp, into the air, and crashed. Another skier raced down the hill, faster and more skillfully than the previous skier. Off the ramp he sailed gracefully: one, two, almost three seconds he hung in the air and then landed safely but not very gracefully.

My stomach wrenched at the thought of flying through the air that long with the sheer terror of agonizing over having nothing under me, with no place to go but down, with no escape from my inevitable crash landing, and my ensuing embarrassment.

Then Father pulled on the reins at the bottom of the hill. "This is going to be a great afternoon to watch the skiers jump, Ole."

FOUR

I swallowed hard again to keep the nausea down. "Sure, Father." *You think I am going to be a great skier. Dear Lord, I need Your help. You said that when we pray that we should ask You to deliver us from evil. Lord, I'm asking. I am begging.* Just then a breeze whipped across the bottom of the slope and stung my face, urging me to move. I climbed into the bed of the wagon to fetch my skis, but the only things under the blanket were supplies from the general store and left-over lumber. "Father, my skis, they are gone!"

"What do you mean, 'they're gone?'" Father stood next to the side of the wagon with an incredulous expression on his face.

I hopped out of the wagon and faced him. "They were there under the blanket this morning. I saw them right there before we left." I lifted the blanket to show him the place they should have been stored. "I am terribly sorry. You had your heart set on watching me leap in the air, but I have no idea what happened to them."

Father appeared confused and shook his head. "Your skis are at home. The skis you saw earlier were Olaf's. I left them at Carl Elk's shop for him to fix the bindings."

"But you kept saying how excited you were to watch me ski today. And how eager you were to have Mr. Elk teach me to follow in the tradition of the *sky crashers*."

Father grabbed both of my shoulders and looked me in the eye. "I never had any expectation of you becoming anything like Carl Elk or any *sky crasher*. I was well aware that we had left your skis at home, so I had not even the slightest thought of watching you ski today or of having you learn from Carl Elk."

"You didn't? You're not disappointed in me?"

"Far from it, Ole. I came here for us, so we could enjoy a couple of hours together, just you and me. Hundreds, even thousands will come here because they are thrilled by the amazing skill and daring of the ski riders. I wanted to enjoy the thrill with you and not with the crowd."

"You did?" *That is contrary to everything I have been thinking.*

"I love you, Ole, and I am fully aware that skiing off of a ramp is torture for you. Why would I expect you to do something that terrorizes you?"

I shook my head, trying to comprehend everything that had just transpired. *Of course! Father loves me! He never pushes me to do anything that is terrible or makes me ill. Why would I think otherwise?* "Father, I am sorry!"

Father pulled me in and hugged me. "I understand. Sometimes fear makes us hear and see things that aren't really there. Just remember, I always want what is best for you."

I hugged him in return. "Yes, and you know me quite well." Throwing my head back, I looked up at the blue sky. "Heh,

heh." I chuckled, and my shoulders shook, jostling Father's shoulder.

Father pulled back a bit and stared at me. "Why are you laughing?"

"I just thought how different today would have been—how much I would have enjoyed being with Father—if I had remembered how much he loves me." Swedish men in Red Wing are not usually demonstrative of their affections in public, but Pappa and I didn't pay any attention to others as we continued hugging each other, wrapping our arms around each other in a prolonged hug.

FIVE

A History of Red Wing's Sky Crashers

Although the story of Ole and his father is fictional, the real story of Red Wing's *sky crashers* is one of which Red Wing, Minnesota is duly proud. A huge boost to the town's Aurora Ski Club can be credited to Chris Boxrud, a businessman who manufactured furniture in Red Wing. He lured Torjus and Mikkel Hemmestvedt to his town from elsewhere in the Midwest with offers of employment at his factory with the use of his factory after hours for making skis.

Before immigrating to the Midwest in the United States and later settling in Red Wing, the Hemmestvedts had been champion skiers in Norway. Subsequently, they were invaluable in teaching Red Wing skiers.

The Hemmestvedts received the nickname of *sky crashers* because the jumps they executed in ski tournaments surpassed anything ever witnessed before in the US. In 1893 an article in the New York magazine, *Frank Leslie's Illustrated Weekly,* featured the breathtaking jumps of Red Wing's Hemmestvedt brothers with a picture of one of them leaping in midair which was said to have fanned enthusiasm for ski jumping, transforming it into a national sport.

For that reason, some have claimed that Red Wing was the birthplace of ski jumping as a national sport in America, though other towns possibly have equal claims to that title.

Red Wing's Aurora Ski Club, one of the first ski clubs in America, dominated ski tournaments for several years. Ski jumping as a sport in Red Wing, however, went on a hiatus following the failure of the railroad companies and the subsequent collapse of the economy from

Taken from: *Sky Crashers A History of the Aurora Ski Club* by Frederick L. Johnson, Goodhue County Historical Society Press, 2003

1893 to 1900. By 1903 the economy and the sport had recovered, and the boys whom the Hemmestvedts had taught carried on the tradition of excelling in the ski jump tournaments. In 1904, near the end of the season in which this story is set, an estimated crowd of between 4,000 and 6,000 watched

200 skiers from several regions of the US compete. All seven of Red Wing's long jumpers finished in the top ten among the entrants in the event, which helped maintain the Red Wing Aurora Ski Club's reputation of having the best jumpers in the US. Their reputation helped Red Wing land the privilege of hosting the National Ski Jumping Championships in 1928 and 1936.

The Bush Street ski jump, shown in the 1905 photo below, reveals what the people standing near the middle of the slope would have seen as they looked towards the very bottom. Though the photo is blurry, you can still distinguish two horse-drawn carriages in the street.

Piercing a Season of Shadows

by Donald Roome

ONE

Marsha isn't usually late, but with last night's blizzard, I wasn't surprised. Manor Care Senior Home is a long commute from Pine Island. Listening in the shadows of my room, I overheard the night shift nurse say that Marsha would need a lot more than just a big snowblower to clear the driveway to her barn. *I hope she finds a way to get in. If one of the other nursing assistants has to fill in for her, it'll likely be a rough morning.*

Knock, knock.

"Good morning, Bill," Nancy announced as she hurried to the closet and grabbed my sweatpants and sweatshirt. Nancy was short and stocky but was one of the older nursing assistants, which meant she knew what she was doing and was able to easily handle my five-foot ten-inch, crippled frame with 180 pounds of mostly dead weight. "Sorry for the long wait," she jabbered, not waiting for a reply because a stroke four months ago had left me unable to form words with my mouth or use my right arm effectively. "We're really short-handed today. I hope you don't mind being on the second shift for breakfast. Phew!

Smells like we should have come in earlier." She dropped the side rail on my bed, cleaned me up, and put on a clean diaper and sweatpants. Then, in one swift motion, she turned me sideways and into an upright sitting position with my feet over the edge of the bed and on the floor. After yanking off my nightshirt, she deftly put my sweatshirt and shoes on me.

Having shivered half of the night, the shoes and sweatpants felt good, yet enduring the cold wasn't what bothered me. The lack of results with my therapy left me feeling that I had fallen in a narrow well a mile deep with nobody for miles around who could hear my voice. *Dear Lord, You have got to rescue me, so I can function like a normal human being.*

Nancy placed my right hand on her shoulder. My left arm had been amputated above the elbow after my arm had been caught in a grain auger on the family farm 15 years ago, which forced me to retire from farming. "Okay, Bill, push your feet down into the floor while I transfer you to your wheelchair."

I nodded, though only my left leg was able to push much. She didn't seem to notice that I was trying to communicate with her, which slammed the lid on any hope I might have had of escaping this morning from this deep well. *At least I can stand on my feet. There's not much else I can do.* Nancy was efficient at her job, and even Marsha wouldn't have had time for pleasantries this morning if she had had to work shorthanded.

Nancy put my stocking cap on and wheeled me out of my room. "Marsha called to tell me to make sure I put your stocking cap on. She certainly takes good care of you." Pushing my wheelchair down the hall, Nancy continued to make polite conversation. "With all the snow we had, your sister, Sally, likely won't make it in. Nothing like a Minnesota blizzard to make us adjust our routines. I just hope one of my sisters is as faithful as your sister if I ever end up in a spot like this."

Nancy left me at a different dining table than my usual for a young nursing assistant to feed me. I didn't recognize her, but she looked tired and uninterested in her job. After 20 minutes or so, some of the kitchen crew started to help feed the residents. Still, most of them seemed distracted with bussing the tables and chatting with each other as Nancy and some of the other nursing assistants returned residents to their rooms who had been in the dining room earlier. An hour later, I still hadn't received any food except two bites of the scrambled eggs.

Nancy stopped by my table, glanced at my plate, and called over to the girl who was assigned to feed me, "Did you feed Bill yet?"

"He wasn't hungry," she replied.

That was news to me. *She had hardly offered me anything at all. If she had, I would have gladly eaten it. Well, what difference does it make? The food here is lousy, anyway.*

Nancy wheeled me into the lounge in front of the TV, along with a few other residents. Fox 9's *Morning Buzz* was almost over, but I was still grateful that Sally had instructed the nursing staff to leave me in front of the lounge TV every morning.

Two

Later, when a couple of the afternoon staff came in early to help the day shift, the hectic bustle lessened, and they seemed to have plenty of help to feed me lunch. Strangely, I didn't want to eat. The nurse came over and asked me if I was feeling okay. I nodded that I was, but that must not have satisfied her because she took my temperature and asked me if I had any pain. I shook my head, which apparently satisfied her because she continued passing medications to the other residents. Then Nancy came and returned me to my room to help me use the toilet. From there, she took me back to the lounge where I could watch soap opera drama and talk show drivel. *Is this what the rest of my life looks like?*

The only other people in the lounge were uncommunicative residents that drooled and stared into space. I had nothing with which to occupy my mind. I wasn't sleepy, so napping wasn't an escape. Consequently, I stared out the window at snow swirling between snow-laden pine trees.

An hour later, I heard Marsha's voice behind me. "Hi, Bill, how are you doing? Are you okay out here?"

I craned my neck around to look at her and then nodded. She still had her boots and parka on, as did a boy of about ten years of age who stood behind her. *Yeah, I am super glad you made it to work.*

"Surprised to see me today, huh?" Marsha grinned, squatting slightly, putting her at eye level with me. Marsha was in her mid-30's and wore her hair in a pageboy that allowed a lock of her brown hair to fall partially over her face when she bent over. "Well, when they finally got around to plowing the road in front of my home, they also plowed the driveway to the barn where I parked my car. I called the supervisor to see if she still wanted me to come in, and she said, 'Sure, come on in.' So... here I am."

Marsha straightened, tucked a lock of her hair behind her ear, and put her hand on the boy of about half her size. "This is my son, Josh. School was canceled because of the snow today, and if you are okay with it, he will work quietly on his homework at the table next to you."

I nodded and studied Josh as he hastily peeled off his hooded jacket. Leaving his boots on, he smiled nervously and waved at me. His nicely trimmed brown hair; clean, yellow, knit shirt; sparkly, brown eyes; and ramrod, erect posture all complimented the grin that, like most kids with Down syndrome, spanned the entire width of his face and radiated a happy perspective on life.

"Josh, this is Mr. Hansen." Marsha put her hand on his shoulder while he leaned toward me, fairly bouncing on his toes. "No talking until your homework is all done, every last bit. Your dad will be here to pick you up in about an hour." Marsha bent enough at the waist that it was hard for him to avoid looking her in the eye. "Mr. Hansen can't talk. For most things, he will call for a nurse with this call light that is here for him." Marsha pointed to a push pad next to my elbow that was connected to a long cord attached to a socket on the back wall. "If he has a small request like changing the TV channel, he might ask you to help him. If he does, he will stomp his foot on the floor. Is that okay?"

Josh nodded.

"You have to ask him *yes* or *no* questions. He can only answer you by nodding his head for *yes* and shaking head for *no*."

After Marsha had left the lounge, Josh kicked off his snow boots and became the epitome of intense concentration as he worked on some basic adding of double-digit numbers. With his head bent over close to the sheet of paper, he spent almost as much time drawing his numbers as he did calculating the answer. He totally ignored the TV.

Thirty minutes later, Elaine, the physical therapist, entered the lounge. "Hi, Mr. Hansen. How are you doing today?" Elaine adjusted the tray table in front of me. "With our staff being short-handed, I am kind of behind schedule. Would it be okay if we just worked on your arm exercises and did them out here in the lounge?

I nodded. I could wait on the leg exercises. Getting my hand normal again was definitely a priority for me in my physical therapy. If my right hand functioned, I wouldn't have to depend on nurses to wash me in places that embarrassed me. The speech therapist had some suggestions for helping me communicate, but I resisted her ideas because she emphasized alternative ways of communicating. I still wanted to speak as I did before, but more pressing was my need to use my hands.

When Elaine laid my hand partially flat on the tray table, I had hoped that my muscles would learn to relax, but for the last few months, they refused to relax enough to extend completely. "I know this is taking a long time," Elaine explained as she gently stretched the thumb out again and then the fingers, "but we have to go slowly." Elaine's cell phone buzzed, and she checked her messages and immediately announced that she would be back in a few minutes. As soon as she released the pressure on my hand, my fingers curled instantly, tighter than before.

I glared at my useless hand. *These sessions are a waste of time.*

"Can I help you, Mr. Hansen?" Josh stood next to me with raised eyebrows and wide-open eyes. I looked over at his sheet of homework and nodded in that direction, doubtful that he was done with his assignment already.

"I'm all done with my homework." Josh grabbed his assignment and lifted it up so I could see it.

What does he expect me to see? I shook my head. *Even his simple math problems are too much of a challenge for me.*

Josh put his assignment back and returned to my side. "I can help you move your hands," he asserted cheerfully. "Just tell me how you want them to move."

I shook my head.

Josh waited a minute, looking at me attentively. "Oh, I forgot. You can't talk. Do you want me to straighten your fingers?"

I shook my head.

Josh paused for a few seconds, looking down at the floor.

"Would you like God to help you so you can relax your fingers?"

I nodded, figuring that might make him happy.

Josh bowed his head and clasped his hands together. "Dear God, please heal Mr. Hansen's hands so he can relax his fingers. In Jesus' name, I pray." Josh waited a few seconds and then looked up at me and asked, "Can you relax them now?"

I shook my head.

Josh slumped for a second and then came closer to my face. "God always does what is best for us, but sometimes He takes longer than we would like."

I nodded, thinking that God better hurry on this one because I was about to give up hope.

"Hi, Josh," a baritone voice from behind me called. A stocky man, around forty years old, wearing a parka, soon appeared next to Josh. "Who's your friend?"

"Hi Dad, this is Mr. Hansen. His hands can't move the way he wants, but I prayed for him, and God is going to heal him."

"Oh...? You did? That's wonderful!" Josh's dad put his hand on Josh's shoulder and turned toward me. "Hi, I'm Tom. I'm glad to meet you, Mr. Hansen."

"Dad, he can't speak. He just answers *yes* or *no* by nodding or shaking his head."

"Oh...." Tom nodded slowly as he smiled. "Well, Mr. Hansen, we have an amazing God who delights in answering prayers that spring from a pure heart, prayed in faith. Get ready to see God do a miracle. My son has a pure heart, and he usually prays what he believes God will do."

I looked at my clenched hand and didn't know what to do with that. *Why hadn't God answered Josh's prayer? Maybe Josh hadn't prayed in faith. I know Jesus can heal, but maybe He is trying to teach me something.*

Josh packed up his homework, put on his jacket, and slipped into his snow boots. He took two steps towards the door and turned to his dad. "Can I see Mr. Hansen again? I just know that God is going to heal Him."

"We'll see, Josh." Tom put his hand on Josh's shoulder and looked at me. "Would that be okay?"

I nodded in reply. *More prayer being offered up for me should be a good thing.*

Josh bounced in place. "Oh, goodie!"

Tom tousled Josh's hair. "We have to check with your mom first."

Shortly after they left, Elaine returned. "Sorry for the interruption." She looked at me with a puzzled expression. "I hope you weren't too uncomfortable waiting for me."

I shook my head. *Maybe God worked a miracle while she was gone.*

Elaine rubbed my arm for several minutes and then gently extended my thumb and then worked my fingers, but my fingers ignored my willing them to relax. I leaned back in my wheelchair and stared at the ceiling. *I give up. This is just a senseless, masochistic exercise. Why is she wasting her time? This is useless.* Then I looked in amazement as my two fingers had relaxed enough, so she could almost straighten them out. My whole body had relaxed, defeated over my inability to progress.

"Yes, look at that!" Elaine gushed over the simple feat. "We have been trying for months to extend your fingers." She pointed at the fingers and grabbed the other fingers to work on them, but immediately all four fingers curled up tight.

Relax, fingers! Listen to me, fingers! Ugh! It's like you belong to another hand—like you are not even mine. I slumped back in my wheelchair, defeated for a moment. Then suddenly, I sat upright again, thinking that surrendering in defeat might have caused my fingers to relax again. As I looked at my hand, reality bashed me on my head. My hand remained as painfully clenched as ever, and while I remained as depressed, my hand stayed clenched too. *I haven't made any progress. What I saw was just a cruel mirage.*

After she rubbed my arm to relax me, she tried to straighten my fingers again, but my fingers stayed clenched tight no matter how hard she tried. Later in the afternoon, Marsha helped me with my therapy, and the lack of results was equally exasperating. Again, no matter how hard Marsha or I tried, my fingers refused to straighten.

THREE

As I lay in bed the following morning and waited for Marsha to arrive and get me up for the day, I mulled over my therapy exercises from yesterday. *What was the point? What happened for a few seconds with my fingers yesterday was a mirage, and my life is nothing but an illusion.*

In the shadows of my room, the bustle of nursing activity from the hallway made me feel like I existed in a separate world. Next to my pillow lay a rubber pad for me to push with the side of my head to make the call light flash at the nurses' station and outside my door. Though my head had nudged it an hour ago, I had no way to tell if the call light was working because the beeper was still silenced from the night shift who had wanted to keep it from waking other residents.

"Good morning, Bill," Marsha chirped as she entered my room. "Time to turn on the lights. Are you ready for breakfast?"

I nodded, glad to see her and more than ready to get dressed and up in my wheelchair, though breakfast food didn't sound very appealing. At least escaping from my bedroom offered a change of scenery that might help me forget how helpless I felt during the morning routine of getting cleaned up.

"You seem kind of down this morning," Marsha said as she set me on the edge of the bed. When I didn't respond to her comment, she continued to talk while she moved me into my wheelchair, dressed me, strapped my arm in a brace as best she could and placed my stocking cap on my head. "Josh told me last night how he asked God to heal your hand. He was quite excited about it. He was positive that God would heal you. Did you feel anything that indicated God might be healing you?"

I shook my head. *All I had was a mirage. My life is just as hopeless now as it has been for the last four months. God may be loving and powerful, but He had other ideas besides healing me from my stroke.*

"You aren't communicating very much." Marsha examined my face and then ran my electric shaver over my stubble. "We've talked before about God and His love and how nothing is impossible with Him if you have faith. We all have doubts at times... except Josh, that is. His faith may be childlike, but it is unflinching and optimistic. He would like to see you again. I know you gave your approval yesterday, but are you sure that it will be all right?"

I nodded. *What would it hurt to have someone with optimistic faith praying for me?*

FOUR

Marsha left me at my usual spot at the table for another nursing assistant to feed me. Although this nursing assistant was more attentive to my needs than the one yesterday, I didn't feel like eating much. When breakfast time was over, Marsha wheeled me into the lounge. "Look at that, guess who is here already!"

My sister Sally was walking in, bundled up in her winter coat and boots. "Hey, Willie, how have you been?" She peeled off her coat, removed her boots, and put on loafers that she carried in a large purse. "Are you glad to see me?"

I nodded enthusiastically. Her presence always seemed to brighten the place.

This morning, however, she looked pale, and her voice sounded a bit husky. Sally sat back on the sofa next to my tray. "I'm sorry. I woke up feeling tired this morning. When I called to see how you were doing, Marsha said that she thought you were discouraged with your therapy sessions."

I looked at her, expecting her to say more. She was staring at the TV, and soon her eyelids began to droop. Shortly, she was breathing through her mouth noisily. Twenty minutes later, Elaine came and greeted us both. Sally jerked awake. "Oh, I'm sorry if I startled you," Elaine said apologetically. "You must need the sleep, Sally. Lay back and rest. I will take Bill into our exercise room and bring him back to you when I am done."

I nodded towards the sofa to encourage her to rest. "No way!" she insisted. "I came here specifically to encourage Willie with his treatment."

Elaine wheeled me into her exercise room, and Sally sat on a chair next to me. This time when Elaine partially extended my fingers during my exercise routine, I tried imagining I was on a tropical beach in an attempt to relax my fingers. "Just relax," Elaine said in a soft, gentle tone as though she was speaking to her newborn baby.

I am trying to relax, but the more I try, the tighter I get. Why won't these fingers relax? After three minutes of straining my brain attempting to relax my fingers, I gave up and slumped in my chair.

"There," she exclaimed, "you did it!" But when she tried to work on my other two fingers, all four fingers contracted again. Elaine remained excited. "You did it. See? It is possible for those tense muscles to relax. Just knowing that it is possible should make it easier now."

I shook my head. *This is just a mirage. My fingers relaxed because I was wallowing in defeat—not because my muscles learned to stop contracting.*

"No, they relax because your muscles *are* able to relax. They just need your cooperation, whether that means feeling defeated or learning to release the tension by positive thinking." Elaine seemed to read my thoughts, which only exasperated me.

How was feeling depressed going to accomplish anything? Am I supposed to live life feeling defeated? How is that going to work?

Elaine looked over at Sally, who was leaning forward in her chair. "She's right, Willie," Sally declared. "They did relax once, and they can do it again." Sally stood and walked next to the tray.

Elaine lifted my hand partially and repeatedly rubbed my muscles, and pulled gently on my fingers to extend them.

With Sally looking at me intently, I was even more desperate to make progress in my recovery. She had almost been in as much trauma over my condition as I had been, and she had always been here for me, doing everything within her power to make me comfortable and healthy again.

You've got to relax, fingers. Okay, give up, body, surrender—you are defeated—why are you still tense? My fingers won't relax unless you give up.

Sally slumped her shoulders as though she was trying to will my body to relax. That only made me more anxious because I was disappointing her. Shortly my anxiety turned to frustration and frustration to anger, and then my muscles stiffened, tighter and more painful than before.

Elaine switched to exercises that I've always been able to do with my legs. After I was done with therapy, Sally wheeled me to my room. She read to me from the newspaper, and normally, I would interrupt her reading by stomping on the floor with my foot to ask her questions, but she seemed too tired today for the effort that yes-or-no questions required. Some days searching for the right question exhausted me as well. Neither of us commented on what happened during my therapy treatment, and Sally left a short while later.

FIVE

The next morning, Marsha informed me that she would be doing my physical therapy treatment from now on because the physical therapist had signed off on the treatment plan and had instructed the nursing staff on how to do my routine. At lunchtime, Marsha told me that Sally had become ill and wouldn't be coming today. Marsha tried to encourage me during my stretching exercises, but the condition of my hand stayed the same. Without Sally to cheer me on, the bottom of the well in which I was trapped became deeper and darker.

Two days later, Sally still was too ill to visit. Marsha asked me in the morning if Josh could visit me. I nodded, thinking it couldn't hurt, and in the afternoon, Josh greeted me as soon as Marsha wheeled me into the lounge. "Hi, Mr. Hanson. I've been praying for God to heal you." Josh rocked on the balls of his feet in front of me and smiled.

I nodded, but didn't feel like smiling back.

He stopped rocking, and he looked at me with a serious expression on his face. "I also asked God if I could see you today. I was so happy when my teacher told me that Mom had called and said that I could walk from school and come here to visit you."

I glanced at him and couldn't resist smiling at him, and instantly, his entire face grinned.

"God answered my prayer about coming to see you today, and He's going to heal you, too."

I nodded. Though I had my doubts, I sure hoped God was listening. My exercises for the last two days had been painful. Marsha tugged on my transfer belt to adjust me in my wheelchair. "Need anything?" she asked. I shook my head, and she tucked a lock of hair behind her ear and looked over at Josh. "When I take Mr. Hansen to his room to do his exercises, you work on your homework, okay?"

"Can I watch him exercise?" Josh stood on his toes and begged. "I want to see God heal him!"

"Mr. Hansen needs to focus on his stretching exercises so that he can get better." Marsha talked as she was walking out of the lounge. "We'll let you know if God heals him." Josh slumped in his chair without saying a word back to her. Then for the next half an hour, Josh asked me all sorts of *yes* or *no* questions: did I like ice fishing, ice skating, ice hockey, had I ever caught any walleye, bass, sunfish, etc. Plainly, he was not making idle conversation. He genuinely wanted to know what I liked and what I had done, for he clapped excitedly whenever I hit upon something he liked or showed surprise when my response was different from what he expected. I couldn't help but continue smiling inside at his enthusiasm.

When Marsha came to take me to my room, Josh asked if he could watch me do my exercises. Marsha looked at me, and I nodded. "Are you okay with doing it here in the lounge?"

I nodded again.

Josh bounced up and clapped. "Oh, goodie!"

"You have to stay in your chair, Josh," Marsha warned and then looked at me. "Are you sure?"

I smiled and nodded. *Having an enthusiastic cheerleader like Josh ought to brighten my day, at least. Besides, he had prayed and had complete confidence in God to heal me, and I certainly needed some God-help.*

"Shall we begin with the hand?" Marsha folded her arms across her chest. I hesitated, but eventually nodded.

She rubbed and slowly stretched my right arm and placed it on the tray table. When she stretched my smaller fingers, they refused to uncurl all the way. "Don't worry," she insisted, "just relax."

Josh stood. "You can relax them, Mr. Hansen. I know you can!"

Marsha pointed to his chair, and he sat.

I grunted. *Come on, fingers, relax! Josh is counting on you.* I studied Josh's concerned expression and then stared out the window as large snowflakes floated down. *God, it's not fair. My failure to improve shouldn't cause Josh to lose faith in You. God, don't you answer the prayers of those with childlike faith? I know You answer prayers that are said without doubt. It is obvious that Josh doesn't doubt. You've got to answer his prayer. You promised in the Bible that if we had faith the size of a mustard seed, we could move mountains. How about moving my fingers?*

Josh suddenly jumped up. "You did it, Mr. Hansen!"

I gawked at my hand. I could hardly believe it. I'd been so busy arguing with God that I neglected thinking about how taut my hand was and hadn't noticed that I had relaxed. "Ha," I laughed as my other two fingers relaxed as Marsha extended them too.

"Look at you!" Marsha exclaimed.

Josh bounced and clapped. "You did it."

I looked at Josh and then at Marsha and chuckled. This was too funny. Josh and Marsha were more excited over that little feat than I could ever be. My chest and shoulders jiggled as I laughed. How could I not laugh? Josh's genuine love overwhelmed me. As I continued to laugh, my fingers stayed extended for a few minutes. Marsha adjusted my hand, and my fingers curled again, but relaxed enough to be straightened again. Josh and Marsha clapped. I laughed harder, but now I was laughing at myself. My hand was doing what I had hoped it would do. My shoulders shook as I laughed harder yet, and tears came to my eyes, blurring my vision. Marsha repeated the procedure a couple more times as I shook my head in disbelief. "Wow," I muttered.

"What did you say?" Marsha grabbed my arm and shoulder.

"Wow," I repeated.

Marsha prodded me. "Say it again."

"Wow!" *I had to be dreaming. Was this for real?* I looked at Josh.

He bounced and clapped faster. "Oh, I asked God to make you speak too," he squealed. "He did it!"

"Wow," I whispered, not so much in amazement, but because I wanted to hear myself say the word.

Josh blurted out, "Say it again!" Josh stopped bouncing and

stared intently. His excitement was contagious even without a cause to be excited. I wanted to speak and tell him how happy he made me. "Wow," I shouted.

"That is a miracle!" Marsha stared with her mouth open. After she finished my arm exercise, she lifted my arm off of the tray table, and I guided my arm around Josh's shoulder and hugged him. He immediately grabbed me with both arms and hugged me back. *He loved me just because that was the kind of person he was. What an amazing kid!* I grinned at Marsha, who looked eager to do more. *I may have tons of work to do to get my hand fully functional and my speech normal, but with Josh and her to cheer me on, that will be more like joyful anticipation than work.* "Wow!" *I can hardly wait to see Elaine's face when she sees what my fingers can do now.* "Ha!" *Imagine what the speech therapist will say!*

DIVINE MOMENTS

BY J. B. SISAM

JASON (J. B.) SISAM is a professional blogger, coach, and author. He helps writers and leaders stay motivated with clear thinking so that they are equipped with tools to find their voice, write their God-story, and succeed in their family, business, and life. He creates believable characters that connect with the heart and delivers stories that resonate with truth. Jason lives in Minneapolis with his wife, Kari and their two children, Amelia and Aaron. Learn more at JasonSisam.com.

You can purchase Jason's books at
JBSISAM.COM

FICTION
Divine Providence
King Lyle and the Purple Dragon
Vengeance at Purgatory | *Jacob Creek Book 1*
Purgatory's Revenge | *Jacob Creek Book 2*

NON-FICTION
Grace: What's So Amazing About It?
Thinking Forward Journal
Focus Up, In, and Out

ONE

Dust settled against the ground as Jackson Tanner pounded the gravel under his cleats. He swung the bat in a circle and connected its tip to his shoe, and watched as more dust fell off his cleats and landed near home plate. A wave of dizziness swept over his body. Beads of sweat slithered down his forehead, forcing his mind to fog momentarily as he pulled the bat over his shoulder. Jackson readied his mind as he stared down toward the pitcher's mound.

"Hey, batter, batter," the opposing team's pitcher said. "I've got a hot one coming in for ya."

Closing his eyes, Jackson willed himself to stay standing. *What was happening to him?*

"Strike two!" the umpire said.

When did the pitcher release the ball?

Jackson stepped back, shook his head, and allowed the dizziness to subside as the catcher tossed the ball back down to the pitcher.

"Are you ready?" the pitcher said.

The pitcher released the ball as Jackson watched in anticipation. He tightened his grip on the bat; the metal squeaked under his gloves. The ball floated left. No chance to hit, giving him one more opportunity to knock one out of the park for the team.

"Ball three!"

It seemed as if the dizziness passed, and his focus returned. Jackson took a glance at his dad, who nodded in approval. Jackson loved that his dad—a former pitcher for the Minnesota Twins baseball team—was his team's coach.

"Hey Tanner, your pro-daddy can't help you get out of this jam."

Jackson stepped up to the plate, dusted off his cleats, and pulled the bat up once more. The count sat at three balls—two strikes. One more chance to gain a hit and end the tied game. Time to bring his friend, Timmy, who sat on third base, home. The pitcher snarled something then released the ball. It was a doozy of a throw. Straight down the middle. An easy target. He'd hit dozens of these balls. Jackson tightened his grip on the bat, dug his left cleat deep into the gravel, arched his body down and toward the ball. A loud crack as the metal bat sang against the ball's assault, transferring its kinetic energy against the ball's leather and sent it deep into right field.

Jackson took off running. He glanced over as Timmy flew toward home. Dizziness collided against his skull. His feet tripped over an invisible stone, and for just a moment, his body flew toward first base before everything went black.

~

Patrick Tanner watched as Jackson's bat collided with the ball, sending it into right field. One of the best hits his son's ever done. A gust of wind blew the hat off his head as he exited the dugout. Jackson ran toward first base just as Patrick made it behind the umpire. Timmy crossed the home plate.

"Nice score! Way to go," he told Timmy. He looked over at first to see if Jackson made base. A group of players were gathered near first base. As Jackson lay motionless on the ground, inches from being safe, Patrick's heart flew into his throat. In three strides, Patrick was at his son's side.

"Jackson?" He checked for a pulse. Relief washed over him as the tiny pulsing of Jackson's carotid artery met his finger. But something was very wrong. Jackson didn't move.

"Jackson!" he called again. "Wake up, buddy."

Two medics pulled at Patrick's arm. "We've got this."

He moved aside as the medics checked his son's vitals. The boy's eyes were rolled back, and drool snaked its way down his cheek. Patrick's eyes blurred with tears as they hoisted Jackson onto a nearby gurney.

One of the medics came over to speak with Patrick. "He's stable. We're not sure what's going on. Might be dehydration from today's heat. Has he had anything to drink?"

Patrick's mind numbed. "Um... Yeah, I make sure we have enough water and Gatorade for the boys." He rubbed his fingers across his face and down his nose.

"Okay. Just checking. We're taking him to Mercy. We'll do a full evaluation and get some fluids into his body. You can follow us."

Patrick nodded, then pulled out his cell phone. "Joan, something's happened at the game. Meet me at Mercy."

Two

Mercy Hospital sat nestled against the Mississippi River in Coon Rapids. Joan and Patrick lived in the nearby city of Champlin, not far from where Patrick grew up. After graduating from the University of Michigan, he was drafted by the Twins, bringing him back home. He played in the league, helping them win a divisional title, and then in his fourth year, Patrick blew out his shoulder, forcing him to retire. How he wished for a brief moment to be back on the mound, knocking off batters.

Jackson lay asleep, looking small in the large hospital bed. Several wires clung to his arm and rose upward toward the nearby monitors. A bag of saline solution hung by a hook, sending much-needed hydration through its long tubes into Jackson's right arm. He looked so small and fragile.

"When will we know something?" Joan asked, walking into the room. She joined Patrick at the hospital a half-hour after he and Jackson.

"I don't know. They took several tests, and now we sit and wait. I need some air. I'll get some coffee and be back."

"Okay," she said. A tear slipped down her cheek.

Patrick lightly kissed her lips, then rested a hand on her shoulder. "I love you. Be back shortly."

Without looking up, she said, "Love you, too."

Once in the hallway, he asked a nurse where he could find some coffee. She told him to look in the cafeteria. They usually had several Keurigs set up and a good supply of coffee for those needing a jolt of caffeine. And a good jolt he needed. He found his way to the cafeteria and quickly found the coffee cups. An elderly man busied himself making a cup of coffee. He had a salt and pepper beard, a green gentleman's hat, and a simple green and black checkered scarf wrapped around his neck.

"Little hot for a scarf, isn't it?"

The man turned and smiled at Patrick with a slight chuckle. "I suppose you're right. I rather like wearing it. Seems to suit my complexion."

"That it does. What brings you here?" Patrick asked, trying to keep his mind off of Jackson.

His rosy cheeks brightened at the question. "Oh, not much. Just traveling through. But, Patrick, I have something for you."

"Okay, but we just met."

The man smiled and pulled out a small card from his wallet. "Oh, nonsense. I've been saving this for you and Jackson for such a time as this. I know you'll need this, and he's going to love it. And the best part, you won't know why you even have this until the moment arrives." He held out the card, and Patrick examined it. To his amazement, it was a baseball card, nothing too special. A current Twins player graced the front: Jason Malone, Jackson's favorite player.

"Who did you say you were again?"

The elderly man smiled. "People have many names for me, but you can call me Nick."

"Okay, Nick. How did you know Jackson would love this car—" The realization that this Nick knew their names staggered his thinking. "How did you know our names? I don't believe we've met?" Patrick was certain he'd never met Nick.

Nick smiled, then let a loud laugh escape his belly. "Oh, I suppose not. But, here's the thing, I know more than you know." Nick tapped a finger against his own head. "I have a lot of thoughts going on up here. They're pretty great. Better than yours. I'll be seeing you around." He handed a cup of coffee to Patrick. "I brewed this for you. Enjoy. Oh, and that card, hang on to it. It's worth more than you know."

"I will, thank you," Patrick said before realizing Nick was already gone.

THREE

When Patrick arrived back to his son's room, his wife, Joan, sat in a chair stroking Jackson's small hand. A lump formed in his throat, and he tried to swallow it back with some of the coffee Nick made for him.

Joan looked up and smiled. "He's still sleeping."

"I take it the doctor hasn't been in yet?"

Shaking her head, Joan tried to hide the tear slipping down her cheek with the brushing of her finger. "Why is God doing this to our little boy?"

Patrick set the coffee down on the window ledge and sidled next to his wife. "Hey there. It's probably dehydration. The doctor said he needed some fluids."

"But why is he sleeping? Shouldn't he be awake by now?"

"He hit his head pretty good, Joan. We'll know more when the test results come back. We shouldn't worry yet."

She shot up from her chair, nearly pulling Jackson's IV out. "Yet? You think there's something wrong with our boy?"

"I didn't say that."

Joan started pacing and tossed her hands into the air. "Well, you might as well have."

A soft knock caught their attention. "Mr. and Mrs. Tanner?" the doctor said, walking into the room. He asked them to sit down. "We finally have some of his blood work back, and we discovered an elevated white blood cell count because he's fighting an infection. So I'm prescribing him some antibiotics to help clear things up. We'll keep him on the IV for the evening because of the dehydration."

Patrick sighed some relief as Joan cupped her hand into his. "He'll be okay?"

The doctor glanced at his notes again. "I want to keep Jackson overnight for observation. Get him rehydrated. I'm also going to have an MRI done as he took a pretty nasty fall, and I want to rule anything out that shouldn't be there." He placed his notes down and crossed his legs. "Do you have any questions for me?"

They asked about MRI results and if they would have them in the morning. The doctor assured them they'd know sooner rather than later, as results are nearly instantaneous. Of course, they'd have to analyze the results before making them known.

After he left them alone, a nurse came to add the antibiotic to the IV fluids. Joan pulled her legs into the chair and reached for Jackson's hand again. "I'm glad he'll be okay."

Grateful it wasn't anything worse, Patrick relaxed. He stuffed his hands deep into his pockets as he stared out the window. "Me too," he finally said.

His fingers poked against the card in his pocket. Pulling it out, he stared at the image of Jason Malone. In the background of the card, he noticed a fan wildly waving at the camera. A small boy lifting his glove into the air sat just behind home plate. His blue Minnesota Twins shirt with the hard-to-miss number 27. His number. Patrick shook his head. He remembered this game.

It was the top of the eighth inning. They were down by two runs. Malone was at bat and nailed a double RBI to tie the game. Probably when the park photographer snapped the picture. Three quick outs, and Patrick Tanner took the mound to give the Twins one more shot at taking the game in the bottom of the ninth inning.

Fifteen pitches in, bases loaded, two outs, two balls, and two strikes. Patrick shook his head at the call for a curveball. He wanted a nice fastball and waited for Joe Mauer to signal the call he wanted. Joe called for a fastball inside. He breathed deep, gathered the ball in his glove, and finding the threads between his fingers, Patrick set up his fastball grip. A quick glance toward second base, then third, and finally set his sights on the batter. His leg pulled up, his body tightened, the leather creaked from his grip, and as he released the ball, something snapped in his shoulder. He cried out in pain as the ball made its target.

"Strike three, you're out!" the umpire called.

Patrick fell to his knees in pain. The team rallied around him as fire raced through his arm. He knew it was bad. Three surgeries later to repair the torn rotator cuff and his career as a professional baseball player had ended.

The card slipped from his fingers at the memory.

FOUR

Two days later, Jackson was back to his usual 10-year-old self. He came plodding down the steps, grabbed a waffle from the toaster, and quickly added butter and syrup to the yellow breakfast treat before finding a seat at the counter.

"Hey, that was mine," Patrick said.

"Sorry, Dad, but I don't want to be late for practice today."

A sudden flash of the other day made its way across Patrick's mind, and he shuddered to see his boy lying on the ball field. Not wanting to upset his son, he let it slide. With a smile, he said, "Okay. Finish that up, and let's get going. I don't want us to be late. We had a rough day the other day, and we're not going to push it."

"Okay, Dad. I'll be good about drinking water."

"Gatorade. It's filled with electrolytes. That's why I want you to drink some today."

Jackson ignored the comment and continued eating.

"Jackson, okay?"

"Fine. Can we go? I don't want us to be late."

Patrick closed his eyes. Jackson had been through a lot the past couple of days. Embarrassment was all his boy could think about. One should never look weak in front of his friends. He poured a to-go cup of coffee and said, "Let's go." As they walked toward the door, Patrick stopped his son by the shoulder and knelt down. "Listen. I know that wasn't fun, and I wish it didn't happen, but all I ask is that you show me a little respect when speaking to me. Do you understand me?"

Jackson nodded. "I understand."

With that and a goodbye to Mom, they were off to the ball field.

Jackson loved baseball. It's all he ever thought about. The sound of cleats digging into the brown gravel, the umpire calling out balls and strikes, his dad cheering on the team from the dugout. Hot dogs, nachos, and the sounds of the other boys getting excited about the next game.

Timmy walked up to Jackson. "Sorry about what happened. I hope you know that you got me home, and we won the game."

"I know. Dad told me when I woke up at the hospital."

"That must have been scary."

Jackson thought about that for a moment. "Not really; I don't remember much. The Jell-O was good, though."

"Was it green?"

"Red. Cherry, I think."

Dad grabbed Jackson by the shoulders. "Enough chit-chat. Time to practice."

They all gathered around home plate as Dad explained

how practice would go today. They would each take turns pitching and throwing to both first and third base from the mound. His goal was to make sure each player could make the play to force an out at the base.

"Even though the last game was good, I don't like sitting at something that's all tied up and waiting for an awesome play to bring home a run. We can't afford to do that each game. We will start losing games if we keep that up. Hands in."

They all put their hands into a giant pile.

"Three. Two. One. Blue Jays!"

Jackson took to the mound, determined not to let a repeat of the other day happen again. He placed his hand into the glove and picked up the ball sitting on the mound. The sun peeked over the dugout, temporarily blinding him. He tightened the grip on the ball and tossed it to Timmy, who was catching.

"Nice job, Jackson," Dad said.

Trying hard not to smile, he wound up again and sent a curveball toward home plate. The ball bounced against the plate and up into the lap of an elderly man holding a cup of coffee, sitting on the bleachers. The man tried to jump out of the way as the coffee splashed.

"Sorry!" Jackson said as he scrunched his face.

The elderly man used his newspaper to wipe away the spilled coffee, walked down the steps, and tossed them both into the trash. He was wearing a green coat, checkered scarf, and a green hat on his head. It looked like something his grandpa would wear.

"Hello, Jackson. It's finally good to meet you in person."

Confused, Jackson asked, "I'm sorry?"

"Oh, where are my manners? My name is Nick. I'm a

friend of your dad's." He offered a wide smile. "Did your father ever show you his baseball card?"

"No."

"Well, I'm sure he has a good reason. It's Jason Malone's rookie card. Pretty neat stuff."

Jackson felt his eyes widen. Jason Malone was not only his favorite player, he was a divisional champion and winner of three golden glove awards. Next to Joe Mauer, Jason Malone was the best player the Twins had ever signed.

Dad finally noticed that he wasn't on the mound practicing. "Hey, Jackson. Who are you...."

"Hello, Patrick."

"Nick. What brings you out to the ball field?"

Nick let out a chortle. "I have a proposition for you. Something I think you'd like."

Dad looked puzzled. Jackson did too, but all he could think about was that baseball card of Jason Malone.

"I'm really sorry, but I've got a practice to run and not much time before another team needs the space."

"I understand. But give your old pitching coach a call. I hear the Twins have an opening for a new pitching coach."

FIVE

That evening, Patrick couldn't help but wonder what Nick was talking about. Leafing through the sports section and browsing on ESPN's website turned up nothing regarding the firing or replacing of the current pitching coach, Ned Young. It didn't make sense. And why would Nick care? Patrick didn't know him from Adam. It seemed odd to have a complete stranger show up twice, concerned with his family, only to share news that no one else knew about. Something didn't add up.

Joan walked into his study and sat in the overstuffed chair. "Want to talk about it?"

"Not really."

"Something's got you all in a tizzy tonight, Patrick. I know Jackson's scare the other day was a fluke, but what if it were more serious than we originally thought?"

Patrick pulled off his reading glasses. "Hey. No need to concern yourself over something that a little fluid from an IV couldn't handle." The baseball card sat on top of his Bible. He picked it up and looked at his friend's image. "I met someone."

Joan looked cross-eyed.

He laughed. "No, not like that. A guy named Nick gave me this baseball card of Jason Malone. Said it's worth more than I know." He paused. "He said the team is looking for a new pitching coach."

Joan shook her head. "Ned's wife, Rebecca, hasn't mentioned anything to me. If you forgot, we're in the same quilting class at First Baptist. I'm sure she'd tell me if anything is going on with her husband."

"Why do you say that?"

"She talks a lot. She's kind of the gossip of the group." Joan laughed, then got serious. "What if you call Ned and see what's up and put some feelers out there."

Patrick frowned. "Joan, I'm not calling up the current pitching coach and asking him if his job is on the ropes."

She got up, rounded the desk, and kissed his cheek. "Think about it. And if you decide not to, then that's okay. At least Jackson will get a nice card out of the deal from this Nick."

Patrick walked up the steps, stood by Jackson's door, and watched his son play the latest MLB game on his Xbox One. The umpire called a strike as Jackson threw a nice-looking curveball. Albeit it was a video game, but the graphics impressed Patrick. His boy lived and breathed baseball, and that made him smile.

The day he got hurt and couldn't play again for the Twins was the worst day of his life. Funny how life seems to throw these curveballs and quickly usher you into a new season of life. For Patrick, he never thought he'd be back at Target Field again until today. This Nick offered him a job to take over his friend's position. It seemed odd he didn't know any Nick on the team's roster.

Walking back to his study, he pulled out his cell phone and dialed Ned. He sat behind his desk as the phone rang.

"Hello."

"Ned, it's Patrick."

The line was silent for a moment. "Hold on." There were some clicking noises and a distant, "*I'm on the phone*," before he came back. "Hi, Patrick, sorry, Rebecca has some ladies over for tea."

"Not a problem at all. Ned, the reason I'm calling, I heard some news, and I'm wondering if you can confirm something for me." What was he thinking? Asking a friend if he was losing his job seemed a little too far as friendships are concerned. But his curiosity was piqued,and Patrick couldn't help asking.

"I'm guessing you're calling about what happened and my stepping down as pitching coach?"

Patrick had no words. Nick was right. "Actually, I heard about it this afternoon from a... friend."

Silence filled the other end of the line. "Malone call you?"

"No. Someone else... hey if you're not in the mood to talk—"

"Listen, Patrick. It's been a long time coming. I've coached for 40 years, and it's time to hang up the hat. I've had a good career. I'm just too darn tired."

"Well, congratulations on finishing out with the best in the league."

Ned laughed. "Have you seen my bullpen? I can't keep these guys in line anymore. They need fresh blood. They need someone like you, Patrick."

Patrick appreciated the compliment, but he'd been out of the game too long to make a good impression. And only playing four years hardly seemed the length someone like the team would need to coach well.

"Listen, Patrick, will you at least think about it? I'm not done until two weeks from yesterday. But they're going to need someone for next year's playoffs. I'm not sticking around that long."

"I'm sorry that it's been a bust of a season, Ned."

"Hey, you can't win them all."

Patrick told Ned he'd think about it and get back to him sooner rather than later.

Six

A week later, Patrick stood on the promenade at Target Field, wondering why he was even taking this meeting with Ned and the current general manager for the Twins, Frank Zillow. Then, looking up at the bronze statue of Kirby Puckett, he said, "Well, big guy, guess I'm probably coming home. Still not sure why they're even considering me, since I've been out of the game for a few years."

Kirby just stood there.

"Guess you're not much of a talker, are ya?"

The gate opened, and out walked Ned Young. For being seventy-two, he looked good. Not super tall, but built like a linebacker, Ned stood five feet, eleven. He wore tan slacks and a dark blue polo with a bright red TC logo embroidered onto the left breast.

"Patrick Tanner. How the heck are ya, my friend?"

They embraced, and Ned knew how to give a hug, like the air being sucked from your lungs.

"I'm good."

"Shall we head up?"

They walked into the ballpark. Several grounds crew members tended to the field, getting ready for the evening's game. Patrick glanced at the screens as they tested some of the videos. It looked like his boys were playing the Dodgers. It should be a good game.

A couple of minutes later, they reached one of the conference rooms. The room wasn't large, but several images of past players, games, and ballpark images adorned the walls. Frank busied himself with some papers as they walked in.

"Ned, Patrick, come on in, take a seat." Frank stood and shook both Patrick's and Ned's hands. "Shall we get to business?"

Patrick's stomach twisted into knots. He never thought he'd join his team again. After blowing out his shoulder during that game several years prior, his dream of being a major sports player diminished to nothing but a dream slipping through his fingers like sand. The fact that the opportunity presented itself all because a man named Nick showed up with Jason's rookie card, eluded his mind.

"Ned tells me you're interested in joining the team again? And given that Ned's retiring, we will need someone in the bullpen who can help us win games. Are you that guy, Patrick?"

Patrick swallowed hard and wiped his sweating hands on his pant legs. "I am honored that Ned thought of me to replace him in the bullpen, and I'd be honored if you'd have me." The sweaty palms subsided. "After my torn shoulder, I never thought I'd be sitting here again having this conversation. And I know my son will be thrilled."

They talked for the next hour about what needed to

happen next, and they wanted him to stick around for the evening game, to which Patrick quickly agreed. He called Joan while Ned and Frank left the room to talk and told her about the opportunity to work for the Twins again. Then, he told Jackson to get his glove ready because he'd be coming to the game this evening.

"Shall we head down and see the boys?" Frank said.

SEVEN

That evening, Patrick settled into the bullpen next to Ned. The thrill of hearing the crowd gather at the gates and slowly make their way to their seats, the sound of popcorn bursting open in the machines, along with the sound of a hard leather ball slapping into a waiting glove while tonight's pitcher warmed his arm filled Patrick's mind. It reminded him of when he sat here as a player. The smell of leather filled the area, and he smiled.

"Are Joan and Jackson here yet?" Ned said as he popped a wad of gum into his mouth.

"Should be here by now." He pulled out his phone and texted Joan. A moment later came the reply that they were in the suite and ready for the game. He told her he'd be up after a while.

"Nothing like it, is there?" Patrick said.

Ned looked off in the distance as if not listening.

"Ned? You okay?"

Ned looked at his friend and smiled. "I'm fine. This game's

gonna be a tough one, but I think my boys will make the magic happen tonight."

He got up and called the pitching team and staff together. "Boys, let's pray."

They took a knee.

"Father in heaven, we thank you for who you are, high and lifted up, name above every name, hallowed be your name. We thank you for this day, and we thank you for your mercies and compassion, as they are made new every morning. Great is your faithfulness. I ask that as we begin this ballgame, you would be glorified by our actions on and off the field. Please, let us win if that is your will. In Christ's name, Amen."

Patrick had never heard Ned pray before. They'd been in the same church for years, but seeing Ned in his element was a joy to watch. He'd never seen anyone pray like that before. He looked around, wishing he had a better prayer life than that, and saw Nick in the stands just above the bullpen.

"Hi-ya, Patrick. Good to see you back here again."

"Nick, good to see you as well. What brings you to the game?"

"Oh, it's an old American pastime. I remember the year you first put on that glove. Boy, that was something special. Your dad was one awesome guy and to take you to Cooper's as a boy to buy your first one. It must have been quite special."

Patrick stood dumbfounded. "What? How do you know that story?"

"Oh, I get around."

"Hey Patrick, who ya talking to?" Ned said.

"I'm talking to...." Nick was gone. "Never mind. I guess I'm talking to myself."

The game started with a bang. The Twins landed two solid and uncontested runs in the first inning. By the time the game reached the fifth inning, the Twins had fallen by three runs, and bases were loaded. Patrick worried they'd have to pull their guy and bring in a new pitcher when Ned looked a little flushed in the face. His friend sat down and wiped his brow with a handkerchief.

"Ned, you okay?"

"Just a little tired. I feel fine. Must have been that last hotdog I ate."

The phone rang.

"You sure you're okay?"

The ringing continued.

"Would someone stop that incessant ringing!"

Ring. Ring. Ring.

Ned looked white. Beads of sweat pooled down his neck.

"Coach?" One of the players asked.

Patrick watched as his friend's head drooped forward as he crumpled off of the chair. Ned hit the floor with a thud.

"Get a medic!"

One of the other coaches grabbed the phone. "We have a medical emergency in the bullpen. Call a timeout. It's Ned."

Eight

Thirty minutes later, they wheeled Ned out of the ballpark toward Hennepin County Medical Center. Patrick had never seen his friend like this before. It didn't look good. The EMTs did chest compressions and oxygen treatment. Once they had a faint pulse, they wheeled him off toward the ambulance.

"Patrick. It's okay. Your friend will be okay."

It was Nick. Somehow he was in the bullpen and had a hand on Patrick's shoulder.

"How did you...."

"It doesn't matter how I got here. It matters because I'm giving you grace as you take the team right now."

"I'm not on staff...."

"Oh, I make ways where there seem to be no ways. Patrick, listen, I know that Ned's your friend, but I've got him, and I've got you. Now, that phone is going to ring. Frank Zillow will be on the other end. He's going to ask you to choose the best candidate to finish the game. Trust me. There are seasons of life and seasons of change. They blow constantly, but if we're patient and listen, we'll see the Father's hand in it all."

"I'm not sure I understand."

Nick laughed and patted Patrick on the back. "Let me put it this way. We never know what turns, twists, and directions life is going to go, but one thing we know is clear: we trust in the Lord with everything inside. By tapping into the Kingdom of God that is within, you'll find your path is already straight."

He pulled out the baseball card from Patrick's pocket. "Look at this picture."

Patrick took the card and expected to see Jason Malone. Instead, to his surprise, the card had his image from his days of pitching. "How is that possible?"

Nick smiled. "What do you see?"

"I see myself."

"What about yourself?"

Patrick's face warmed. He didn't feel much of anything. The concern rising in his chest for Ned flooded his mind.

The phone rang.

"I see someone who was out of his league then and out of his league now."

Nick smiled again. "What else?"

The phone continued ringing.

"I see a failure. Someone who should have had a full and wonderful career as a pitcher, destroyed by one stupid muscle that tore."

The phone still rang.

Nick held up the card so Patrick could get a better look at it. This time the card was Patrick as he looked now. Tired, worn out, unfulfilled. "Do you know what I see, Patrick?"

Tears welled in Patrick's eyes. "A little league coach who is past his prime and should give up on his dreams because they'll never happen."

Nick took off his glasses and tucked them into his green jacket. "You know, there's a story of a man who gave three of his workers some cash. To one, he gave a dollar, to another five, and yet another ten. Then, he went away on a business trip and asked them to do what they liked with the money.

"The one with ten simply invested it and used it to double his returns, to which now he has twenty. The one with five did the same, but the one who had the one dollar stuck it into his pocket and did nothing with it. When their boss returned, they each gave an accounting of their stewardship.

"The one with the single dollar told his boss that he knew he was a hard man and gave him back the dollar. He wasted his opportunity to do something with what his boss had given him. The boss fired him and gave his dollar to the man with the original ten dollars."

Patrick wasn't following.

"Patrick, you've been given a gift. You see your son's dehydration, your torn shoulder, and Ned's heart condition as a bump in the road. I see it as an opportunity that brought you here for this moment. When the moment arises, what are you going to do?"

The phone's ringing stopped.

"Are you going to take a chance and trust God, or are you going to leave your dollar in the pocket and never invest it and see your season of life change? What are you going to do with your talent?"

The assistant coach handed Patrick the phone. "It's Frank."

Patrick continued looking at Nick, wondering who this gray-bearded man was. He took the phone, all while not taking his eyes off Nick.

"Yeah?"

"Patrick, good. I have a question for you."

NINE

"I need a man of your talent back there. It's not that I don't trust the rest of the pitching staff. I do, but they're not familiar with the pressures of making decisions during the game. They're young, and they're looking to you. One of them said as much. I want you to call the shots back there and send the best out, so we can win this thing for Ned. Can I count on you?"

Nick said, "I believe in you."

Patrick didn't know what to say. He'd been out of the game too long. He had no clue how to run a pitching staff. But, they had four innings left, and if he could get them out of this alive and give the batters a chance to bring this thing home, what choice did he have?

Seasons come, and seasons go. But living life and taking chances seem to be what God ordained man to do. Nick stood there smiling. Patrick still had no clue who this man was and why he gave him so much attention. The question lingering in his mind was this: *Can I do this?* Was now the time to make a change and take a chance on himself?

"Patrick? I don't have all day!"

He swallowed hard. "Frank..."

Nick smiled.

"I'm your guy."

"Great! Get your guy, call the shots, and send him out."

After he hung up the phone, Patrick walked over to Nick. "Why me?"

A warm radiating smile filled Nick's face. His eyes sparkled with delight. "Patrick, you'll do just fine. I'm proud of you." He handed Patrick the baseball card, which now showed Patrick holding the glove his father gave him. "Always remember who you are and who you are called to be. You've got this, and I've got you."

Patrick looked down at the card as tears blurred his vision. "Thank you." But when he looked up, Nick was gone.

"Coach, what's our next move?"

Patrick shoved the card into his pocket, straightened his ball cap, and turned to face the pitchers. "Okay, boys. Let's focus on winning this game for Ned. I'm sure he's just fine, but we have a game to finish." He looked around the bullpen. "Justin, you're warmed up. Let's send you out."

The young pitcher looked terrified. "First game?"

He nodded.

"Listen, you'll do just fine. Go out there and get our batters back up to plate."

"Yes, sir."

Patrick picked up the phone, nodded for the door to be opened. "Sending up Justin." He watched as the young boy walked into the outfield and toward the pitcher's mound, remembering the first time he stepped foot onto the field all those years ago. Nick was right. Take a chance and see God do amazing things in your life.

The team did great. Even though they didn't win, Patrick was convinced he was set in that bullpen for such a time as that moment. No one knows what God's going to do next, but Patrick was certain that if he trusted enough, had faith to step out into a new season, he'd be all right, and God would do the rest.

Sophie's Season of Change

by Barb Winfield

Barb Clobes Winfield has always known she liked writing. As an elementary principal, she had many opportunities to write professionally. It wasn't until retirement that she found the Minnesota Christian Writers Guild (MCWG). Joining MCWG has expanded her skills and broadened her horizons. This led to writing her first fiction. What fun!

Barb has 2 daughters, 6 grandchildren, and 2 great-grandchildren. The newest addition to her life is a rescue cat named Sophie. Many of Sophie's personality traits appear in the fictional piece in this book. Sophie really does put her toy mice in her food dish and say "Hmm" as she thinks and makes decisions throughout her day.

Barb is currently working to finish a non-fiction book on how we (as a nation) are inadvertently teaching our nation's children how to be violent.

You can reach Barb at BWinfield@msn.com.

ONE
SOPHIE MEETS A FRIEND

"Hi, my name is Sophie," I said to the cute little creature sitting on the floor in front of me. She was gray with pink felt ears and a small rope tail that was also pink. "What's your name?"

"Skittles," she replied.

"Just what kind of creature are you?" I asked. I leaned forward to sniff her. She was soft to the touch and made of gentle gray fabric. I could smell the stuffing inside her; it had a bit of a catnip smell. She lay very still, but she could talk.

"I am a mouse. That is what they made me to be. Is that okay?"

"Are you a real mouse?" I asked. "You can talk, so you must be real. I need a real friend to play with. It gets lonely being the only non-human creature around here."

"I must be real, I can hear you, and I am hungry. Is there anything to eat around here?" Skittles asked.

"I am a cat. I have some dry cat food my human put in a dish right there," I told her. "Do you want to eat that?"

"That might be okay. I have never had cat food to eat. At least it is food. But Sophie, I can't walk over there; how will I get there?"

"I can carry you," I replied. "I can use my mouth to carry you if you don't mind."

"That would be great. Just don't drop me in the water dish. Ahhh, I was worried about your teeth there for a minute. Thanks for the ride." Skittles sighed as she settled in and took her first bite. "This food tastes really good."

It was dark outside, and my human was fast asleep in the bedroom. I can see so well in the dark, and night was a time I could check things out in the house at my own pace. Best of all, this was a time to visit and play with my little toy mouse friends. They are the only friends I have. Thankfully, my human brought several little mice home in a package when she came home from a trip to Walmart one day. They have been a great source of fun and frolic. I bat them around with my paws and retrieve them with my mouth. Skittles was a new little mouse, and I had not met her before. Besides that, I noticed the slightest movement when I first looked at Skittles. That was why I said "Hi" to her. I had not met a toy mouse that talked and could see me before this one.

Skittles was chomping away on a piece of dry cat food that had a salmon flavor to it. She took a moment to ask, "What is the name of your human? Have you been with your human since you were a baby kitten?"

"Oh no," I replied. "Her name is Mommy Bea. She refers to herself as 'mommy' when she talks to me, and I hear others call her 'Bea.' This is the fourth place I have lived. I like it here. I have not always liked where I lived."

"What do you mean?" asked Skittles.

"Let me tell you about it while you eat; I can sit right here next to the dish and tell you the story if you like." I moved closer to the dish and sat down where I could see Skittles and be sure she was comfortable as she ate.

Two

Sophie Shares Her Story

The first place I lived was with Tall Lady Mama. She came to the place I was born and picked me up when I was just nine weeks old. She took me to where she lived, and she always said, "Come to Mama." I heard others call her Adele, but since she always called herself Mama with me, I thought of her as Tall Lady Mama because I had to look so far up when I first met her. I liked her smell, and she liked to hold me on her lap. I would purr, and she would pet my fur. I liked to kiss her hand and take a nap right there. And then I would get spunky, jump down, and run around as fast as I could. That was fun!

Tall Lady Mama had a cat tree that I could climb upon. I like tall places where I can see everything. I could tell she really liked me because she had lots of special things for me, and we had fun together. I even pounced on her hand sometimes and pretended to bite her hand. Sometimes my sharp teeth broke into her skin a bit. I didn't mean for that to happen, but a cat has to play, you know! I guess my teeth are sharper than I think.

Skittles was enjoying listening to my story. She could only remember rolling out of a machine and being placed in a package with nine other little felt mice. Aside from the rack holding the other packages of mice at that Walmart store in Elk River, this was the first place she'd seen since being created. "Tell me more," Skittles said. "I want to learn more about your life. It sounds nice."

"Sure. I lived with Tall Lady Mama for lots of birthdays. Beth and Sadie would come to see her. Beth would call Tall Lady 'Mom.' Beth was busy all the time she was at our house. At first, Beth and Tall Lady Mama cooked food together and sat at the table and told stories and laughed. They would laugh when I ran by fast or batted at their hands. Then, they would pick me up and talk to me. I liked the attention."

I checked to see if Skittles was still eating while in my dish. And then I continued.

"Sadie was younger than Tall Lady Mama and Beth, like me. Maybe she was a kitten, but of the people kind. But just like me, she kept growing bigger. Sometimes Sadie would play with me and pull a ribbon I could chase. I loved that. Sometimes, as she got older, she was not so nice to me. She didn't like me near when she was playing with her phone or doing that stuff with books that she called homework. I know I am cuter than those books, so I would go sit on them and lay down on them. Sadie didn't like it when I sat on her books, and she would yell at me. Sometimes she even hit me to make me get down. I still did it every time she had her books at our house."

I took a deep breath as I thought about the next part of the story.

"After a long time, Tall Lady Mama didn't seem to feel so

well. She had to lay in bed more and more. She was always happy when I came to her bed to see her, but she didn't get up to sit in her chair in the living room or play with me like she used to do. Then one day, Tall Lady Mama had someone there to take care of her, and me too. That lady washed the dishes and cooked some food. She vacuumed the floors and cleaned up things. She even washed some clothes and my blankets sometimes. She stayed each night in that other bedroom at our house. I called her 'Cooking Lady.'

"Beth came over lots of times too. She tried to be happy and sing a little as she brought some soup to Tall Lady Mama, but I could tell she was sad. Skittles, did you know that cats can tell when people are sad? When Beth sat down, I would sit on her lap to help her feel better."

Skittles looked up from her lunch and into my eyes and asked, "What is sad? What does sad mean?"

I paused to think how I could explain the meaning of sad to Skittles. "Hmmmm. Let me think. Well, let's pretend that you and I could play and I could bat you and carry you, and we could have fun together. But if I couldn't find where I left you or if you got stuck behind something, then I would feel sad until I found you."

"Oh," Skittles replied. "Is sad what I feel when I want to move by myself, but I can't?"

"Yes, that is a good example of sad." I nodded, and then I continued the story.

"Anyway, I didn't know it then, but everything was about to change. One morning, Tall Lady Mama didn't wake up and call for me like she always did before. I went to check on her, and she didn't move. I didn't know what to do, and I was sad and scared. I started to meow as loud as I could. Maybe Cooking

Lady would come and fix this. I could hear her in the kitchen. I meowed again and again as loud as I could. Finally, I went into the kitchen and meowed and ran in circles next to where Cooking Lady was pouring some juice. Cooking Lady looked at me and said, 'Sophie, just what are you doing?'

"I ran into Tall Lady Mama's room and jumped up on the bed. I made another loud MEOW! Cooking Lady came to the door and looked at me. Then she looked at Tall Lady Mama and walked closer to touch her. Cooking Lady said, 'Oh no!! I need to get some help!' She left and called someone on her cell phone.

"I laid down on the bed by Tall Lady Mama's legs, and I put my chin on her leg. I thought maybe I could help her feel better. In a few minutes, a man and a lady came into the bedroom, pulling a bed and with a bag of things in their hands. They pushed me onto the floor, and then they touched Tall Lady Mama and put things on her arm. They told Cooking Lady that they had to take Tall Lady Mama to the hospital. Then they each got on one side of Tall Lady Mama and lifted her onto that bed they could pull. They pulled her out of the room and right out of the house. I tried to follow, but Cooking Lady said, 'NO, Sophie!' and pushed me away from the door. I ran and looked out the window, and I saw them put my special Tall Lady Mama on a truck and shut the door. Then that man and lady started that truck, and some bright lights came on and started to blink, and I heard a loud screeching sound that went up and down. The truck drove away fast and took Tall Lady Mama right away from me."

"Oh no," Skittles said. "What happened next?"

"Cooking Lady made another call on her cell phone, and I heard her say, 'Beth, the ambulance just took your mom to

Mercy Hospital. She was not conscious this morning when I went to check on her. I will meet you there.' Then Cooking Lady grabbed her coat and left the house. I sat by the window and watched her go away too. I was all by myself, and all I could do was wait."

THREE

A Season of Change

Skittles was still sitting in my food dish. She had eaten two full pieces of my cat food, and she looked down to choose a third one to eat. She picked a piece that tasted like garden greens. As Skittles started to chew, she looked up. She must have seen the tear I felt running down my cheek.

"Why is there water trickling down your face, Sophie?"

I used my paw to brush the tear away. "The water that comes from your eyes is called tears. People and creatures get those when they are either really happy or really sad."

"Oh, does telling this story make you really happy or really sad?" Skittles asked.

"Memories of Tall Lady Mama make me sad," I sighed. "I miss her. That was the last day I ever saw her.

"I was all alone, and I sat and looked out the window for hours and hours over the next three days. I ate very little and took naps on a chair with a clear view of the door. No one came. On the third day, I realized there were only a few pieces of food left in my dish. Tall Lady Mama or Cooking Lady usually put out fresh food one day at a time. My water was also very low. What would I do when there was no more food to eat or water to drink?"

Skittles asked, "Was there any way for you to get more food or water by yourself?"

"No," I answered quietly. "The thing I was most worried about, however, was Tall Lady Mama. Why couldn't that man and lady bring her back home in that truck with the lights and noise? Where was Cooking Lady? She was always here every day. And where was Beth? Beth came here often, too. I heard Cooking Lady talk to Beth on her phone about them taking Tall Lady Mama to the hospital. What exactly is a hospital? Why did they want to take Tall Lady Mama away from me? I wanted them to bring Tall Lady Mama back."

"This story is getting scary," Skittles said in a shaky voice. "I can tell you were worried and scared. What did you do?"

I heard concern in Skittles' voice, and I looked at her as I continued.

"Well, on the night of the third day, I was napping in the chair when I heard people at the door. When the door opened, Beth and Sadie came in and turned on the lights. Beth came and picked me up and asked if I was okay. All I could say was, 'Meow' but I was glad to see them.

"Beth said that Tall Lady Mama had died at the hospital and that she would not be coming back home anymore because she is in Heaven now. I wanted to shout at them. I had so many questions. What is a hospital? What does it mean to die? What is Heaven? Why would Tall Lady Mama want to go there and not take me along? All I could say was 'Meow.'

"Then Beth and Sadie started talking to each other as I gathered up my things. Beth told me that I was going to live at

Sadie's apartment with her now. She said that Tall Lady Mama wanted Sadie to have me and all my things.

"'NO!!!!' I tried to say. But all that came out was 'MEOW.' I did not want to go with Sadie anywhere. But I didn't get a choice. They got a couple of boxes and put my toys and a blanket in one. Then they put my dishes and food in another box. 'Meow,' I said. What about my cat tree? But they must not have heard me. Beth put me into my cat carrier and shut the door. Then she picked up a box and my carrier and headed out the door. Sadie grabbed the other box and followed her out. Sadie shut the door and locked it while Beth unlocked the door to the car.

"I did not like what was happening. Every time they put me in that cat carrier, I had to go see the 'Vet' and get a shot or something else awful. I started to cry, 'Meowwww, meowww, MMMEEEOOOWWWWWWW!' They just kept going. They put the carrier with me in it into the back seat and got in the front. Beth started the car and drove away. Beth and Sadie were talking, but I was still crying. I guess they didn't hear me."

Skittles stopped eating and looked at me. Her little face seemed to pucker, as if she was feeling sad and scared too. Skittles asked, "What happened next?"

FOUR

I stood up and started to pace in a circle near the dish where Skittles was sitting.

"Well, in a little while, Beth pulled the car into a place and stopped. I got quiet because I wanted to see what would happen next. Sadie grabbed me in the carrier and a box while Beth locked the car, and we went into a big door in a big, tall building. The room we entered had lots of lights. Sadie walked to some metal doors at the back of the room and waited for Beth to join us. The doors opened, and we got in a very small room, and they turned to face those doors. Then they pushed some buttons and said we needed to go to the fourth floor. It felt funny as this room gave us a ride up to the fourth floor.

"We walked down a hall, and Sadie used her keys to unlock a door. Sadie opened the door, and we went into this place. Right away, I did not like the smell. It did not smell like the house where I lived with Tall Lady Mama. I had smelled this before. Then I remembered it was when Sadie came to visit

Tall Lady Mama. It didn't smell good to me, and it certainly didn't smell like home. Sadie set my carrier on the floor and opened the door. I sat right where I was; I did not want to come out right then. Sadie and Beth unloaded the boxes and put my food and water in my dishes. I was happy to see I had both food and water again.

"Sadie already had a litter box there for me. Sadie said, 'Sophie, see this - let me show you your litter box.' Sadie reached into my carrier and grabbed hold of me. I did not want to come out yet. I was scared. So, I bit Sadie's hand - hard. She yelled 'OUCH' and called me a dumb cat. Then she saw some blood on her hand and slammed her hand on my carrier. Beth said, 'Sadie, calm down. All this change is scary for Sophie.' But Sadie used her mad voice and shouted, 'All this change is hard for me too!'

"Beth suggested they just let me be in my carrier if I wanted to stay there. She said she thought I would come out when I felt more comfortable. I thought to myself, 'Right, and that will not be until everyone is in bed and sleeping. Then I will feel safer and can check it all out.'

"After a little while, Beth said she was tired, and she was going home now. She got her things and left. As soon as she left, Sadie kicked my carrier hard and walked out of the room. I stayed right in there, and I was shaking. I didn't like it at Sadie's place."

Skittles stopped her munching and looked at me. "Were you sad? You told me what sad means. Is that what you were feeling?"

"Hmmmm. I guess I was more scared than sad. I didn't like being alone with Sadie. But, more than anything, I just wanted to go home to be with Tall Lady Mama. Why did they say she was in Heaven? Why couldn't I go there too?

"I heard Sadie get ready to go to bed, and her lights went out in that room where she went. I waited a long time before I dared come out to get a drink of water or use the litter box. I needed to know she was not going to hit me like she hit my carrier.

"Finally, in the dark, I stuck out a leg. I wondered if it was just as warm out in the room, and I wanted to be sure I was safe. So I pulled my leg back in and leaned forward to stick my nose out into the room. Then I really got brave and stepped out–all the way out. That was when I saw him."

"Saw who?" Skittles shouted. "Who was there, and was he going to hurt you?"

"I was not sure, but he was pretty little compared to me. I must have jumped and looked afraid because he said, 'You look scared. I won't hurt you. I am just a cockroach looking around for food at night.'

"'Do you live in this place with Sadie?' I asked in utter amazement. I could not imagine anyone wanting to live with Sadie. He looked harmless. He was small and had six legs, and the antennae on his head kept wiggling in every direction. 'What is your name?'

"'I don't think I have a name. People just scream if they see me, so I like to hide until it is dark and they are sleeping. No one ever calls me by a name.'

"Then I guess I just have to name you. Your name is Fred,' I said. 'My name is Sophie, and I am a cat. I am here because my Tall Lady Mama died and went to Heaven. Now I have to live with Sadie, and I don't think I am going to like this. You go ahead and find some food; you can have some of mine. My dish is near the kitchen. I am going to check this place out. Maybe I will see you tomorrow night, Fred.'

"With that, I walked toward the kitchen, sniffing everything I could find along the way. I ate a couple of pieces of food and had a drink of water. Then I decided to use the litter box. I sniffed and walked and checked everything in the entire apartment until it started to get light outside, then I went back to my carrier and crawled in for a nap.

"Eventually, Sadie got up and wandered into the living room, where the carrier still sat on the floor. Sadie looked inside and saw that I was asleep in there. Sadie said, 'You stupid cat. Are you still in that carrier? Are you going to sleep all day?' With that, Sadie lifted the back end of the carrier and dumped me out onto the floor.

"I ran and hid under the sofa—way in the back. Sadie left and found a yardstick and started poking it under the sofa to make me come out. I moved around, trying to avoid getting hit. When I saw her look the other way, I ran out from there and into her bedroom. I had checked this place out last night, so I knew the best places to hide were in a closet or under the bed. There was a tall bookcase in the living room also. Maybe I could jump up onto the top from the chair and find a safe place there, too. All day long, when I saw Sadie come into a room, I left that room and went to look for another place to hide. I was quiet, and I was fast. Every once-in-a-while, Sadie would pick up the stick and try to push me out of a hiding place. This went on for four days. I had to eat and drink water and use my litter box at night.

"Then on the fourth night, I came from a hiding place to get something to eat, and I saw Fred, the cockroach, again. He was munching my food too. Fred looked at me and asked, 'Are you okay? I have been watching you run from one hiding place to another. What are you going to do?'

"I sighed and sat down. 'I have no idea what I can do. I just know I do not want to stay here and live like this.'

'Have you tried prayer?' Fred asked.

'Prayer? What is prayer, and how can that help?' I asked.

FIVE

Fred stopped his nibbling and looked me straight in the eyes, and said, 'All you have to do is say the name of Jesus. God created the earth and all the creatures on it, including you and me. Jesus is God's Son, and Jesus came here to live and show us how to live and love each other.'

'Wait a minute,' I said. 'Jesus came to Sadie's apartment to live? Did Sadie try to hit him with a stick too?'

Fred said, 'No, Jesus came from Heaven to save all the people on the earth from their sins.'

'"Hmmmm.' There was that word 'Heaven' again. Maybe this was how I could join Tall Lady Mama. 'What do I need to do?' I asked Fred. 'And just how do you know about God and Jesus and Heaven?"'

'Sometimes God sends an angel to help those on earth who are in trouble or sad and lonely. You need to talk to Jesus, just like you are talking to me,' Fred explained. 'Tell Jesus what you are worried about, give your cares over to him, and he will help you. Just remember to believe in Jesus. You need to have faith that he will provide for you and that he loves you.'

"I went back to my cat carrier, and I crawled in there. Fred said I should just talk with Jesus and give my cares to Him. So I said, 'Jesus, I need to talk with you, and I need Your help. Tall Lady Mama went to Heaven, and now I live with Sadie. She doesn't like me and tries to hit me, and I don't know what to do. Fred says I should have faith and that You love me and will provide for me. So here I am, asking for Your help in this present time of trouble.'"

"Wow!" Skittles said, with her eyes wide and bright. "Did it work? Did your prayers work?"

"I guess so, but not how I expected my prayers to work. The next morning, Sadie came out of her bedroom and saw me sleeping in the carrier. She dumped me out again, but this time, I ran for her foot and nipped her on the back of her ankle. Then I ran and hid as fast as I could run."

"'Owwwwie, owwwie, you dumb cat!' Sadie yelled as she examined her ankle. 'That's it! You don't like me, and I don't like you, so I am taking you to the Humane Society today. You and all your stuff are out of here as soon as I can get ready and get you there!'"

"What is the Humane Society?" Skittles asked.

"I didn't know what the Humane Society was either. Sadie got ready and then went looking for me. I was hiding in the closet in the hall, but she had seen me run into there. Sadie snuck up and grabbed me and stuck me in the cat carrier, and shut the door fast. I was scared, and I meowed as loud as I could. She carried me to the car and put the carrier and me in the back seat. Sadie started the car and drove off. We drove for a long time. I meowed some, but I remembered that I had prayed for Jesus to help me. Maybe this was my help. I decided to pray some more. I prayed as hard as I could, and I asked Jesus to take me to Heaven with Tall Lady Mama or to find me a new home."

"Did Jesus do that?" Skittles asked.

"Well, not at first. The Humane Society was a place for cats and dogs and rabbits and other animals to stay while the people there tried to help find a new home for them. With me in it, Sadie took my carrier into the Humane Society. She told them her grandmother died and willed her and all her stuff to her, but this was not working. She did not want me at her house. She had some important papers with her that she gave to them, and I heard her say my name was Sophie. The man there was nice, and he told Sadie they would take good care of me while they looked for a new home for me. Sadie gave them my bag of food and paid them some money, and she left."

Skittles looked at my eyes to see if there was a tear again. Seeing none, she asked, "Were you sad again?"

"No, I was just glad to be away from Sadie," I replied. "I decided to pray some more."

Six

Sophie Finds a New Home

"The man carried my carrier, with me in it, down a hall and into a room where there were several wire cages. I peeked out, and I could see that almost every cage had a cat in it. One cage had two cats in it. The man went to an empty cage and opened the door. Then he put some fresh food and water into that cage. He even added a pan with some kitty litter in it. All the while, he was talking to me. He kept saying my name, and he was using a calm, quiet voice. He told me I was going to be okay now. He said, 'Sophie, we are going to look for a new home for you. This is where you will stay for now. You are safe here.'"

I stretched. Telling this story was taking a while. But Skittles didn't seem to mind.

"I stayed in that cage almost all the time, every day. Sometimes they took me out to a room with shelves and places for a cat to climb. I would climb up and sit on a shelf there. They put other cats in there with me, but I just ignored them. I sat on the shelf and prayed for a new home for me.

"One day, the man that worked at the Humane Society

came in and told me that a nice lady called and asked questions about me. He said they put my picture online on Pet Finder and told people about me. He said he hoped this would turn into a new home for me. Some more days went by, and every day was the same. I didn't eat very much. I couldn't run or play, so I just sat and prayed some more.

"Then one day, the man came in and said, 'Sophie, that lady that called about you last week is coming to meet you. She is looking for a cat, and she thinks you might be the right one. She will be here at 2:00 tomorrow afternoon.'"

"Wow!" Skittles exclaimed. "Were you excited?"

"Well, I wanted to meet her too. I knew I could sniff her hand and tell if she liked me. I decided to pray some more.

"The next day, the Humane Society man brought a lady into our cage room and opened the door to my cage. He said, 'Sophie, this is Bea. She came to meet you.'

"I leaned forward and sniffed the lady's hand while I stayed in the back of my cage. Her hand smelled safe. Then I stepped forward toward her, and she reached out her hand for me to get a better sniff. I decided to walk close and give her hand a kiss. The lady must have liked me because she told the man that she thought this would be a good match. They closed the cage and left the room to do some papers. I heard her say she had asked God for a cat that needed a new home.

"Soon they came back, and the man picked me up and put me into the carrier the lady had in her hand. I don't like carriers, but I was quiet. Then the Bea lady took me to her car, and we left for the trip to her house. That is when I got really scared, and I started to cry MEOW again. I cried, and I cried. Maybe this idea of praying was not such a good one. Where was I going, and what was going to happen to me now?

"After a long time, the Bea lady stopped at an Arby's to get some food. I got quiet and just watched. Her eyes looked kind. She kept telling me I was going to be okay. She said I was going to live at her house now. She said I didn't need to cry anymore. Then she looked up toward the sky, and she prayed out loud. She asked God if she should give me a piece of the sandwich. A tiny piece of meat fell over her fingers right then, so she shared it with me. I never eat human food, but I ate this little bite. I felt better. It looked like she wanted to take care of me. Besides that, she prayed too! I decided to keep quiet, and I only said a tiny meow all the rest of the way to her house."

Skittles was amazed. She said, "This is quite a story! Is that how you got here?"

"Yes," I answered. "When we got to her house, she had a new cat tree and lots of toys for me. Every morning we sit down in her prayer chair, and she gets out her books. She knows I am cuter than books, so she puts one on her lap that I can lay on while she reads out loud and prays. I sit there, and I pray too. Sometimes I purr, and I kiss her hand. Sometimes we play."

"I like this house," said Skittles. "Can I stay here with you and Mommy Bea?"

"Sure, you can," I said. "I have been praying for a friend."

Thank You!

We hope you have enjoyed this collection of heartfelt stories from many of the talented authors at the Minnesota Christian Writers Guild. Our goal is to bring the gospel message of Jesus Christ to a world in need of hope.

Life is full of many seasons. Seasons of change, of pain, of growth, and also seasons of learning to be still in spirit.

There is a time for everything, and a season for every activity under the heavens.

— ECCLESIASTES 3:1 (NIV)

As you look around at God's amazing creation, it's easy to see that he has made everything beautiful in its time. God has set eternity in the human heart. His desire is to see his creation happy as they show others his eternal goodness.

Life is tough. As I was growing up, my father often said,

"God has not promised us a life of ease, but he has promised us a life of victory."

Nothing could be better than to enjoy our life and to enjoy our work. Why? Because our eternal father can bring to fruition all that we desire.

What do you desire? King David wrote in Psalm 37:4, "Take delight in the Lord, and he will give you the desires of your heart." Commit your way to the Lord by trusting in him, no matter what life brings into your path.

It is for this reason that James wrote, "Consider it pure joy, my brothers and sisters, whenever you face trials of many kinds, because you know that the testing of your faith produces faith (James 1:2–3, NIV).

My prayer as you have read this book is that you've been encouraged, and your countenance has been lifted. This book has been a labor of love so that you can find hope and faith in Jesus Christ.

Today is your chance to find the hope you've been looking for. Jesus gave his life on a cross so that we might be saved. His life wasn't taken from him, but he laid it down willingly so that we may live with hope, life, and joy.

For God so loved the world that he gave his one and only Son, that whoever believes in him shall not perish but have eternal life.

— JOHN 3:16 (NIV)

If you've never asked Jesus into your life, here's a simple prayer you can pray:

Jesus,
I cannot live this life apart from you. I know that I have tried to
do things my own way. I am done trying my way and I'm ready
to live your way. Thank you for sending Jesus to die for my sins
so that I may have eternal life. Please come into my life and
bring me hope, life, and joy
Amen

In this prayer is good news. The Bible says your old life is now gone, and you are a new creation in Christ Jesus. His life has become your life.

Next, go tell someone your decision and find a good Bible believing church to help you grow in your new faith. Your life is about to change forever, and I am so happy for you!

Welcome to the family!

**Here is a website to help you
begin your new journey!
https://peacewithgod.net/**

Thank you for reading this book and supporting the art of writing. We hope you enjoyed it! If you'd like to learn more about the Minnesota Christian Writers Guild, visit our website at MNCHRISTIANWRITERS.COM. We can't wait to meet you.

Writing for Christ,

Jason B. Sisam
President